TAGGED OUT

TAGGED OUT

Joyce Grant

James Lorimer & Company Ltd., Publishers
Toronto

James Lorimer & Company Ltd., Publishers acknowledges the support of the Ontario Arts Council. We acknowledge the support of the Canada Council for the Arts which last year invested $24.3 million in writing and publishing throughout Canada. We acknowledge the Government of Ontario through the Ontario Media Development Corporation's Ontario Book Initiative.

Cover image: iStock

Library and Archives Canada Cataloguing in Publication

Grant, Joyce, 1963-, author
        Tagged out / Joyce Grant.

(Sports stories)
Issued in print and electronic formats.
ISBN 978-1-4594-1075-6 (paperback).--ISBN 978-1-4594-1076-3 (epub)

I. Title. II. Series: Sports stories (Toronto, Ont.)

PS8613.R3653T33 2016   jC813'.6   C2015-907194-1
                                                C2015-907195-X

James Lorimer & Company Ltd., Publishers 317 Adelaide Street West, Suite 1002 Toronto, ON, Canada M5V 1P9 www.lorimer.ca	Canadian edition (978-1-4594-1075-6) distributed by: Formac Lorimer Books 5502 Atlantic Street Halifax, NS, Canada B3H 1G4	American edition (978-1-4594-1078-7) distributed by: Lerner Publishing Group 1251 Washington Ave N Minneapolis, MN, USA 55401

Printed and bound in Canada.
Manufactured by Webcom in Toronto, Ontario in January 2016.
Job #527570

For Bennett,
and for all young baseball players.

CONTENTS

1 THE PITS

Nash Calvecchio stepped up to home plate, his mouth set in a scowl. The sun caught one of the few shiny spots on his scuffed blue helmet. He'd struck out once this game and he wanted revenge.

"*Strike!*" the umpire cried, balling his hand into a fist.

Nash — known to his teammates on the Blues as *Gnash* — moved out of the batter's box and glared at the ground.

He looked over at Coach Coop, who calmly patted his chest and then his arm and his ear. It was the signal for "take." Coop was betting the pitcher would throw wild. But *not* swinging went against everything Gnash was about. He wanted to crack that ball as hard as he could — so hard it would make the fielder's hand sore.

"*Steeeee-rike!*" the umpire called again, this time with a bit more feeling.

The coach had been wrong. The pitcher had thrown a strike. And what had Gnash done? He'd stood and watched it go by with his bat up in the air. Like an idiot. Well, not this time. Gnash didn't look over at his coach to get another useless signal.

Gnash stepped back into the batter's box. He knocked the head of his bat on the left corner of the plate, and then the right. Then he straightened up and raised his bat. He loaded up, shifting his weight onto his back leg. In a split second, the ball came screaming in at him ... wide of the plate. Gnash swung wildly, catching a piece of it with his bat. But it was a small piece, and the ball spun crazily up into the air.

"*MIIIIIIIIIINE!*" yelled the other team's catcher, jumping to his feet. He snatched off his mask and helmet so he could see the ball as it came down.

Gnash had started running when he'd made contact, but he knew it was hopeless. Halfway to first base he heard the *thwack* of the ball as it landed in the catcher's mitt.

"Out!" yelled the umpire.

Gnash scowled on his way back to the dugout, gnashing his teeth in the way that had earned him his nickname. He avoided eye contact with Coach Coop, who was standing with his arms crossed.

"Gnash, you've got to take my signs," the coach said. "You need to wait for the good ones. That guy can't find the strike zone."

Gnash's response was a grunt. He threw his helmet noisily onto the bench. He looked around for his hat and his glove and took a long swig of Gatorade.

"Nice one, Gnash," said his teammate, Miguel. Miguel spat on the ground and shoved his cap down onto his head. "Way to go — you're oh for two now."

Gnash kicked the metal fence, which clattered noisily. "Crap!" he said, loud enough for the parents in the stands to hear.

The inning went downhill fast after that.

Most of the players on the Toronto Blues Pee Wee baseball team had been playing together for years in an inner-city park called Christie Pits. The baseball diamonds — there were three of them — were located at the bottom of an enormous depression that had once been a gravel pit. It was a park with a lot of history, and not all of it good.

"Christie Pits was where my dad mixed it up with those Jewish kids in 1933," Gnash's grandfather had often told him. "Man, him and his brother couldn't stand those kids. Those kids thought they were better than us Catholics."

Gnash had heard the story of his great-grandfather and the famous Christie Pits riot a million times.

"Dad was one of the Pit Gang boys," Gnash's grandfather would tell him. "One day after a ball game — well, those Jewish kids got their butts kicked, is what happened."

Gnash had even looked it up once, when he'd wondered whether his grandfather was exaggerating. But it had been right there in Wikipedia.

Gnash scowled and looked out of the dugout. He tried to picture ten thousand hoodlums there, filling the Pits with their hatred for people who were different. But he couldn't imagine his favourite park that way. The Pits he knew was a safe, warm place. It was where he went to get away from turmoil.

"Six hours," Gnash's grandfather had told him, shaking his head. "Six hours they fought with clubs and bare fists. And then the cops came through on horseback. My dad said you shoulda seen them. They hauled all the kids offa each other."

The top of the inning brought Gnash back to the ballgame. He ran out onto the field with his team. They threw the ball back and forth while they waited for the first pitch.

"Hey, Sebastian! Heads up!"

Gnash saw Sebastian snap his head up and pivot his body toward the sound of the voice. The stocky catcher scowled behind his mask at a ball that was coming in fast from third base. The ball bounced hard off the ground near Sebastian's foot and into the tip of his mitt.

"Good block!" said Tami, at third base. She cringed. "Sorry about that."

"Yeah, no problem," mumbled Sebastian, clearly irritated at Tami's mis-throw. He stood up and whipped the ball to second. "Second base, coming *down!*" he yelled. Miguel caught the ball and then sent it back to Raj on the mound.

Raj was at least a head taller than anyone else on the team. He was also taller than anyone else at school or, for that matter, any twelve-year-old in the neighbourhood. He weighed exactly twice as much as the team's right fielder, Lin, who came up to his chest.

Raj threw bullets. However, while a lot of kids feared Raj's pitches for their speed and power, plenty more feared them for their inaccuracy. Gnash always said that batting against Raj reminded him of those firing squads from the movies — except it was the guy doing the firing who was blindfolded.

"Play ball!" said the umpire.

It was the top of the final inning, and the Cardinals were up by seven runs, thanks in part to Gnash's unfortunate performance at the plate.

"Don't count yourselves out yet," Coop told the kids who were slumped on the bench in the dugout. "Look at last week's games — 15–11 ... 8–3. Anything can happen — we're still in this."

"Yeah, sure, we can win it," growled Gnash. "If they suddenly start running around the bases the wrong way!"

"Hey, maybe that would turn the score back, like when Superman flies around the Earth and turns back time," said Sebastian, neatly catching the ball that Gnash suddenly whipped at him from the dugout. Sebastian laughed and adjusted his mask. He tossed it back and then crouched down into position behind home plate.

On the mound, Raj put the game ball into his glove

and leaned down into his pitching stance. He turned his head to look at Miguel on first base. Miguel nodded and smacked his hand in his glove. Raj nodded back and then looked at Sebastian behind the plate for the sign.

Sebastian showed two fingers and then pointed to his left thigh.

Gnash saw Raj shake off Sebastian's sign and ask for a new one. Sebastian gave the sign for a fastball. Raj nodded.

The pitch was intended to be fast and inside — and in a way, it was. It was practically *inside* the batter's *jersey*. The Cardinal managed to turn his back to the stray bullet, so that it didn't hit anywhere it would do real damage. But all of the parents in the stands heard the sickening thud and they made a collective gasp.

"That's gonna leave a mark," Gnash heard Sebastian mumble as the batter limped down the first-base line to take his base.

"Shake it off, Raj!" Gnash yelled to the mound as the pitcher took his stance again.

But Gnash could tell that Raj wasn't going to be able to shake it off. Nailing the batter had unsettled him. The pitcher's face fell and he looked down at the ball in his glove. Raj wasn't going to be able to shake it off at all.

The next victim from the Cardinals was a gangly left-hander with a long, blue ponytail. She didn't look thrilled to be facing Raj. Still, she gamely stepped into the batter's box and raised her bat above her left shoulder. She glanced nervously over at the stands, where her mother gave her a shaky thumbs-up.

Even the umpire was beginning to look a little rattled.

Raj didn't discriminate between boys and girls. He was an equal-opportunity hit-by-pitch-er. The girl walked to first on the first pitch, rubbing her ankle and pushing the batter ahead of her to second base.

Once the Cardinals got into scoring position, that was what they did — score. Over and over again. The batters that Raj didn't walk or hit managed to get around the bases on overthrows by the infielders. One stray ball went into the equipment shed, something that none of the Blues could have done on purpose if they'd tried.

"We need another game ball!" the umpire called to the coach.

"Get up there and find some, will you?" Coach Coop barked at Lin, who zipped out of the dugout to scour the long, scrubby grass on the slopes of the Pits, looking for glimpses of white amid the brown and the green — a hopeless task.

Meanwhile, Raj was looking for a way out of the inning. He glanced several times over at the bullpen. He looked relieved to see Tami warming up.

Coach Coop held up one hand and strode toward

the first baseline. "Blue!" he said. The umpire yelled, "Time!" and everyone knew that Raj's inning was over. Out on the mound, Raj handed over the ball to the coach like a farmer handing over a rotten egg. Tami jogged out to the mound and waited until the two had finished their conversation. Then, she took Raj's place.

The "good job" applause for Raj was polite but sparse as he left the mound but he didn't seem to hear it. It was clear from the look on his face that all Raj heard was his own voice in his head telling him he wasn't good enough.

"I can't pitch," Raj said to Gnash as he slumped down on the bench in the dugout. "I suck. Everyone's laughing at me. I'm never going to make double-A."

Gnash looked at Raj. Although he wanted to find some words that would make his friend feel better, he knew there was nothing he could say. *Besides*, thought Gnash, *Raj is right — he sucks.* He didn't see how Raj would ever have a chance at moving up from A to AA the way he was pitching.

The two boys watched the rest of the game in silence.

2 NEW KID

"Trade you half an egg for half a salami," said Raj, holding out a bun toward Gnash and slopping egg salad onto the table.

"Gross," said Gnash.

"I'll trade," said Tami, ripping her sandwich in half. She took a swig of milk. "Geez, I can't wait to play the Pirates."

The Parkhill Pirates were an uptown team that hailed from one of the snobbiest neighbourhoods in the city. Worst of all, Parkhill was a team the Blues hadn't beaten in years.

"You mean you wanna *beat* the Pirates," said Raj.

"Yeah. I wanna get those rich kids on the field," said Tami. "And then I wanna crush them."

"Then we *shall*!" said Sebastian enthusiastically, in a British accent. "Crush them, we shall!"

The teammates laughed.

"Hey, Sebastian, is that the new kid?" Tami asked in a low voice. She nodded her head toward a boy eating a sandwich two tables over.

The five teammates turned as one to look over at a boy in a black t-shirt and jeans.

"Huh. That guy looks really gay," said Gnash.

The others looked at the boy more closely.

"Oh yeah," sneered Gnash. "He's definitely a *ho-mo-sex-sssssual.*" Gnash drew the word out like a hiss.

"Keep your voice down, you jerks," said Raj.

"Why?" asked Gnash, loudly. "You in *love* with him or something?"

There were snickers. Raj picked up a potato chip and threw it at Gnash, who made kissing noises with his lips. He picked the chip off the table and tossed it into his mouth. "*Mrth, zmm* — boyfriend!" he said.

"Bite me," said Raj, flicking chip crumbs off his shirt.

The boy in the black t-shirt stared down at the sandwich he was eating, and chewed slowly. He wiped his mouth with the back of his hand, and stood to throw his garbage into the bin as he left the cafeteria.

"Hey, I bet that kid really *is* gay," said Gnash.

Several of them nodded.

Raj watched the boy head out of the double doors of the lunchroom. He put his hands flat on the table and pushed himself to his feet.

"I'm gonna go ask him," he told Gnash with a smile.

"Huh?" said Gnash. "You're gonna ask him if he's *gay?*"

"Sure," said Raj. "Might as well find out, eh?"

Tami stared at the pitcher. "Raj!" she called. "Hey, Raj, you can't do that — come back!"

But Raj was already through the doors, following the boy. Gnash pushed out from behind the table and scrambled after Raj, beckoning to the others to come. They followed in a close clump behind Gnash. When he stopped suddenly at the doorway they bumped into him, sending him sprawling out into the hall.

"Get back, you morons!" said Gnash, pushing everyone back inside.

"Hi," he heard Raj say to the boy in the black t-shirt.

The boy stopped, not turning around.

"Hi!" Raj repeated. He held out his hand. "I'm Raj!"

The boy turned around and looked at Raj. Gnash ducked his head quickly backward to avoid being seen.

"Ouch!" said Sebastian, rubbing his forehead where it had just connected with Gnash's skull.

Gnash looked at him accusingly. "I said get back," he snarled. Then he turned his attention back to the conversation in the hallway.

"I'm Jock," said the boy, holding out his hand. A thin, white leather bracelet on his wrist stood out against his dark skin. "At least, that's what my friends call me." Jock shook Raj's hand, not meeting his eyes.

There was a pause.

"Well, I'm supposed to go to the office . . ." Jock said, shrugging.

"Do you go here now?" asked Raj.

"Started this morning."

"You in 8-7?"

"Nope, 8-6. Mr. Joyman's."

"Oh yeah, he's great. Hilarious," said Raj with a smile. "Have you met him yet? Have you seen his clothes? I think he gets them from Goodwill. Really, I'm pretty sure."

"Yeah. I did notice that," said Jock, looking down at the clock on his battered cell phone. "Well, I'm supposed to . . ."

"Oh, yeah, the office. You'd better hurry."

Jock started to walk down the hall.

"Hey, what's *that* stand for?" Gnash heard Raj ask him, pointing to the letters *CPS* printed in red, white and blue on Jock's t-shirt.

"Crest Public School," said Jock. "It's in New Jersey. You wouldn't know it." Now the boy was sounding irritated. "Any more questions?"

"Well, yeah, I do have one more as a matter of fact," said Raj. "But it's a big one."

Gnash couldn't believe what he was hearing. Raj was actually going to ask him if he was gay!

"What is it?" Jock stopped walking. He turned to look Raj directly in the eye, as if steeling himself for a blow.

Raj stopped walking too, and paused. Then he smiled.

"My big question is: Are you planning on walking the entire way around the school?"

Jock looked confused.

"Because the office is that-a-way," said Raj, smiling. "I'll show you."

The two boys turned and started walking toward the office. Gnash and the rest of the team dove back into the cafeteria and into their seats at the lunch table. Gnash slouched down in his chair, propping up his head casually on one hand. Sebastian linked his hands behind his head and leaned his chair back, whistling tunelessly.

"Don't look over at them!" Gnash hissed to his teammates, as Raj and Jock passed the open cafeteria doors. "Pretend we're still eating!"

That wasn't hard for Tami, who hadn't finished her sandwich yet. Sebastian, who'd already wolfed his down, grabbed an empty chocolate milk carton and pretended to drink from it.

"Don't worry about them," Gnash heard Raj say, pointing at the cafeteria. "They're total idiots."

"Yeah, so I've noticed," said Jock.

"Hey! That's, that's ... *slander*!" said Sebastian loudly, getting out of his seat.

Gnash shoved him back down. "Shut up, you idiot! They're going to know we're listening!"

In the hall, Raj raised his eyebrows at the other boy.

"Well, they're pretty loud," said Jock.

"True," said Raj, smiling over at his friends.

"So, the office is just down here," Raj said to Jock. The two boys walked down the hall and then entered the office.

Gnash got up from the table and crunched his paper lunch bag between his hands. He dropped it in the recycling bin and then sped out of the lunchroom. He caught up to Raj, who was just coming out of the office.

"Hey," Gnash called. "Hey!"

Raj stopped and turned.

"Oh, man, Raj," said Gnash. "What the heck?"

"What?" asked Raj, his eyes wide with fake innocence.

"You didn't *ask* him — did you?"

"Why wouldn't I?" asked Raj. "We want to know, don't we?"

"Yeah, I guess," said Gnash. "But it just seems . . ."

"What, like none of our business?" asked Raj. He grinned broadly.

Gnash stared at him, and then backed up a step. He came forward and slapped Raj hard on the back. "You loser!" he said gruffly, realizing that Raj had been stringing them along the whole time.

"Don't tell Tami, okay?" said Raj, stopping at his locker. He chuckled. "I'm sure she thinks I asked him."

"Man," said Gnash. "You goof," he said, rolling his eyes.

★★★

Gnash took his seat in Math class and stared out the window at the playing field. The teacher was a blur at the corner of his eye, her voice a dull drone.

The door to the classroom opened and all heads turned to see Jock standing in the entrance, looking around the room for a seat.

Without stopping to address the boy, the teacher waved her arm vaguely toward an empty desk beside Gnash. Jock sat down and looked around at the students on either side of him, giving one girl a "hello" nod.

Gnash ignored Jock to stare out the window at the birds circling the parking lot next to the kids' playground. He watched as a motley grey pigeon pecked at a McDonald's wrapper.

A group of kindergartners was clustered around a tall blue slide. A tiny, mop-headed boy in a Mid-Toronto Public School t-shirt stood at the top, looking at his classmates with wide eyes. He was clearly too scared to go down.

"Sit on your butt," Gnash muttered. "Sit on your butt!"

Gnash was still watching the scene outside, wondering if the boy would go down the slide, when he slowly realized that the other students in his class were looking at him. The teacher's droning had stopped. Gnash slid

around in his chair to face the front of the room. "Uh
. . . pardon?" he asked.

A familiar feeling washed over him. To Gnash,
school was always uncomfortable, always boring and
above all, always embarrassing. Then, Gnash was saved
by the bell. The teacher looked at the clock above the
door and saw that time was up. Gnash sighed with relief. But, "Mr. Calvecchio, before you leave, can I see
you for a moment?"

Gnash looked down at his desk. What had he done
wrong? Nothing! He looked out the window at the
boy again, who was sitting on his bottom now. He held
the teacher's hand as he slid slowly, carefully, down the
slide. He had a big smile on his face.

Gnash clenched his fists and opened them. He did
it again. He took a deep breath and shoved his books
into his bag. He got up from his seat and went to talk
to his teacher.

3 AMERICAN DREAM

The team watched Raj, pedalling as fast he could along the sidewalk that circled the deep valley that was Christie Pits. They were practising in the diamond at the bottom, throwing long balls in pairs.

Gnash shaded his eyes with his hand to watch as Raj left the sidewalk and steered toward the grass. Raj picked up speed on the steep hill. Most people who came to the park used the long, paved path with the railing to get down the hill, but Raj was late so he wasn't playing it safe. He was heading straight down. His ancient orange bike was a blur as he swept down the hill, faster and faster. Raj gripped the handlebars, trying to angle his bike to keep his balance. The team watched the pitcher slide the last twenty metres down the crunchy grass, before he slammed into the concrete equipment shed at the edge of the field.

Ditching his bike, Raj pulled his glove out of his backpack and ran to join his teammates on the field.

"Hey, Raj," Tami yelled, running toward him.

"Thank goodness you're here. I'll throw with you — I've been stuck with Coop."

Coach Coop sneered at her good-naturedly and tossed the ball to Raj. "You can do your penalty laps after long-toss," he said to Raj.

Raj grimaced, but he knew there would be no getting around the punishment for being late to practice.

Raj and Tami had only gotten in a few throws when they, and the rest of the team, were called over to the second-base line by the coach. The team sprinted in and gathered around Coop. Each player went down on one knee to listen to the pre-practice briefing.

"Okay," said Coop. "First — Raj, six laps for being late. Second, you may have heard the rumours, and they are true."

"We're getting a new kid?" blurted Sebastian.

"Yes," said Coop.

"What position is he gonna play?" asked Sebastian.

"We haven't figured that out yet," said the coach. "We're going to try him out and see what he's got. He was an all-star in the States."

The words "States" and "all-star" got Gnash's attention. He leaned forward, past the coach, to catch Miguel's eye. When he couldn't get Miguel's attention, he turned to Tami and punched her lightly on the arm. "All-star," he said.

"Yeah," she whispered back. "American!"

Gnash and his friends knew that in the States

baseball was practically a religion. An American all-star player was double-good.

"We might have a shot this year," Gnash whispered to Tami.

"All right," said Coop. "Don't get too worked up. This team has twelve players. Not one, not two — twelve." But the team had a bit more energy as they ran back onto the field.

Gnash watched as Raj started his laps, touching each pole as he ran by it. The year before, the team had gotten some help from a volunteer running coach.

"I use that guy's advice whenever I have to run poles," Raj had told Gnash. "He was an Olympian. He didn't medal, but still. I wrote down everything that guy told me, and I go back and read it all the time."

Raj seemed to be using that advice now. "Head down, arms loose, power from your legs and core," Raj was saying out loud as he ran. Raj touched a pole. "Head down." *Step-step.* "Arms loose." *Step-step.* "Head down." *Step-step.* He touched another pole. "Arms loose." *Step-step.* Gnash had to admit it seemed to be helping Raj.

When Raj finished his final lap, Coop was waiting for him. "That's amazing," he said to Raj. "How'd you do that?"

"Do what?" Raj puffed, his mind still on his form.

"You were going really fast," said Gnash, beside the coach.

"I don't know," said Raj. "Maybe there was a tail

wind or something." They both smiled. Raj grabbed his glove and ran out to the field.

But if Raj was in good form, the same couldn't be said for the rest of the team. They looked like the Bad News Bears on an off-day. Coop was hitting grounders to the team. But thanks to a cycling club that had come through the day before, the infield was bumpier than a camel with the mumps. Clods of dirt stopped the grounders, and divots caused the balls to fly up in every direction.

"Ow!" complained Gnash, as a baseball bounced out of a hole and smashed into his chin.

"Get in front of the ball!" yelled Coop, in an effort to rein in the chaos.

Sebastian was still wearing some of his catcher's gear. As he ran for a grounder, his foot caught the edge of one knee pad and he went sprawling onto his stomach. The ball rolled to a stop in front of his outstretched glove. He put his face in the dirt in mock agony as the rest of the team tried not to laugh out loud.

"Sebastian, is there a reason why you're wearing your pads?" yelled the coach.

"Sheer laziness?" offered Gnash, sweetly.

"I . . . I knew we were doing infielding next," Sebastian tried to explain, still sprawled on the ground.

". . . and you didn't feel like changing," sighed Coop. "All together now . . ." he said to the team who yelled on cue: "FOUR LAPS!"

Four laps for laziness was the standard punishment.

Sebastian got to his feet and brushed the dirt off his jersey. He started sprinting to the outfield to do his laps when he was stopped by his coach.

"TAKE OFF YOUR PADS!" Coop yelled, exasperated. "And what are the rest of you looking at?" he asked the team. "Let's get back to work!"

Sebastian had a good sense of humour and by the second pole, he had clearly begun to see the lighter side of his situation. His trademark grin reappeared.

Even Coop couldn't help but smile as Sebastian ran in to the dugout after he'd finished his laps. He patted Sebastian on the shoulder as he went past. "I'm giving you crap about being lazy and you were *still* going to do those poles without taking off your gear, weren't you?"

"Coop, you know me so well," said Sebastian, grinning.

Coop rolled his eyes.

"Get on second base," he said. "Gnash can catch. Wouldn't want you to have to put your gear on again!"

Sebastian ran out to second, laughing and thumping his glove. No one took Coop's punishments too seriously. *After all*, thought Gnash as he started to put Sebastian's kneepads on to fill in for him, *Coop was just like the rest of the Blues — only a little bit older.* And age didn't necessarily make you wiser.

4 HE'S OUT!

The team was still giving Sebastian a hard time about his laziness the next day at school.

"Hey, Sebastian," said Gnash, "want me to help you take your jacket off?"

"Yeah," said Tami. "Maybe we should carry you to English?"

"Get on!" said Raj, sticking out one hip as if he wanted Sebastian to climb onto his back for a ride. He was just off-balance enough for Sebastian to shove him into a nearby locker. Raj landed with a hollow, metallic clang.

"Get out of here!" said Sebastian. "And I want you to know that I hate each and every one of you," he added. But it was clear that he meant the exact opposite.

Raj pushed himself away from the wall and turned to his locker to get his English books. All this horsing around was going to make him late, he complained, as Tami and Sebastian sped off to class ahead of him.

"I can never work this stupid lock," Raj whined, frantically spinning the dial.

He's Out!

"What's the problem?" asked Gnash.

"It's rusty," said Raj. "Everything I own is old and rusty."

"I'll stay and help you, but we're both gonna be late," said Gnash.

The two boys looked at each other — then grinned.

"Yeah, as if *that's* ever a concern," Gnash laughed.

They were still fighting the lock when the bell rang. There was no one in the hall now, since being late carried a demerit point. Gnash had enough of those already. He was thinking about telling Raj to give up on his books and go to class when they heard voices down the hallway. There was a thump as though someone had crashed into a locker.

The two ran, following the sounds down the hall. They rounded the corner and spotted a group of boys.

"Hey!" Raj yelled. Two of the boys ran off, laughing meanly.

Gnash loped toward the third boy who, he was surprised to find, was Jock.

"What happened?" he asked. Jock looked pale and shaken.

"Nothing," said Jock, turning away. "Nothing. Leave it."

"Seriously, what was going on?" asked Raj.

"Just leave it!" Jock snarled. "Can't you just leave it?! You know, I never asked you guys to be my guardian angels. Do you mind?"

Gnash paused for a minute, trying to think of a comeback. Raj interrupted before he could work up a good one.

"Actually," said Raj, "yes. We do mind. And so should you. This is messed up."

"Okay, fine," said Jock, glaring at Raj. He inclined his head toward Gnash. "You want to know why I hate this school? Why don't you start by asking your jerk *friends!* They're the kinda guys that make my life harder."

Jock grabbed his books from his locker and stalked off toward his class.

Gnash, whose English class was in the opposite direction, was left to stare after him. Was this guy accusing them of something? Were some of his teammates involved in what they'd just seen? They hadn't looked like kids from the team, but they'd run off before Raj and Gnash had gotten close enough to see them clearly.

Gnash was deep in thought as he and Raj walked into their English class and were handed demerit slips by their teacher. They were marked with one demerit point for being late, and one for being without their binders. Gnash crushed the note into a ball and stuck it in his desk, where it joined a slew of others.

Gnash couldn't concentrate on grammar. How could he possibly care about nouns and verbs when he needed to know what his friends were up to? He wondered about Jock, too, and soon he couldn't contain his curiosity. Making sure the teacher wasn't watching, he slipped his battered cell phone out of his pocket. It was a hand-me-down from his cousin. It looked nasty but it worked just fine, especially after he'd figured out the password for the school's Wi-Fi.

He turned off the sound so it wouldn't beep and he typed "Jock" and "Crest PS" into the search engine. The first entry was a list of hockey players, with photos and stats. He scrolled through them, not seeing the face he was looking for. From the back of his memory, Gnash recalled that Jock's last name started with a C. He typed "Jock," "Crest PS" then "C" and hit Enter. This time, it was a baseball roster . . . and the first kid on the list was the now-familiar boy in the black t-shirt. His face looked a little younger, but he was recognizable.

Jock was listed as J. Christobel, a shortstop, number 18. There was no other information, but it was definitely him. Now, at least, Gnash had a last name to go on. He went back into Google and typed "Jock Christobel 18 New Jersey" and hit Enter.

There was one relevant article — a news story in the *New York Herald*. The headline was "Young All-Star Athlete Comes Out" and it was accompanied by a picture of Jock in his baseball uniform.

"Holy crap," said Gnash under his breath. "He *is* gay."

Jock was *gay*. It explained a lot, Gnash realized. And he wasn't afraid to talk about it, even in a newspaper article! Gnash shook his head. He couldn't imagine talking to a reporter about being gay. He couldn't think how a guy would even *know* that he was gay.

Gnash tried to get Raj's attention to tell him what he'd just discovered when he realized that Ms. Grimshaw was next to him. He blinked and looked up at her, trying to get his bearings.

Ms. Grimshaw just stood, silently holding out her hand, looking as if she was prepared to wait all day until she got what she wanted.

Gnash closed his phone and put it into her hand.

"Thank you," she said, handing him another demerit slip.

When she turned back to the board and couldn't see him, Gnash crumpled up the demerit and tossed it into his desk with the others.

★★★

The sun shone hot and bright over the Pits that afternoon. The players were trickling in for their practice before the game. They gathered at the back of the dugout and dropped their bags. They were preparing for battle against the Parkhill Pirates. Raj ditched his bike by the equipment shed and walked over to Gnash. Coach Coop was nowhere to be seen.

"That's weird," Raj said. "Where's Coop?"

"Who cares?" sneered Gnash. "We know the warm-up drills — we'll do them ourselves. Let's go!" Gnash sprinted off to the outfield with a ball and his glove.

"C'mon, who's throwing with me?"

Raj sprinted out to join him, and threw what was meant to be a long ball. It landed three metres in front of Gnash. "Well, at least it was in a straight line," said Gnash.

"Shut up and throw the ball," said Raj. "Anyway, we always start closer than this. C'mon, close in."

Gnash came in a bit and threw the ball back to Raj. He caught it neatly and threw it back, this time perfectly at Gnash's chest. Tami and Miguel joined in and soon after that, the rest of the team was lined up, all throwing balls to each other. They stepped back and threw again, and stepped back again until they were farther and farther apart.

Soon, Raj and Tami were the only ones who could throw the distance without bouncing the ball or throwing a massive rainbow. But that didn't mean that Raj's throws were accurate. Gnash was doing a lot of running and fetching.

"Okay, let's start to bring it in a bit, guys!" Gnash said to his teammates. Relieved, they started to pull in closer to their throwing partners.

Off in the distance, two tall figures broke through the sun that was now low on the horizon. They looked like action heroes striding out of the sunset toward the ball diamond.

"Hey, you guys!" said Sebastian, excited. "That's got to be our new guy!"

Gnash looked up and shaded his eyes to see if he

could make out who it was. They were both wearing baseball uniforms.

As the two baseball players came closer, Gnash recognized Coop but he still couldn't see any of the other figure's features. They both had baseball gloves, and each carried a baseball. Coop was talking but his companion wasn't responding.

Suddenly, Gnash had a terrible feeling about who the new player might be.

"Holy cow . . ." said Tami, as the pair got closer.

"It's . . ." said Sebastian.

"The gay guy," said Gnash, through clenched teeth.

"*Jock*," corrected Raj.

Jock did not look happy.

"C'mon over, guys," said Coop. "I'd like to introduce Jock — your new teammate."

The team took a knee in front of Coop. Jock got down as well, still looking grim.

"Jock's from . . . uh . . ." he trailed off and looked at the new boy.

"New Jersey," Jock said, tersely.

"New Jersey, right. Welcome, Jock. He'll play at short for this practice — now, I want everyone working hard today. Get pumped and let's go. Poles!"

"Shortstop!" blurted Gnash. Why was Coop giving the new kid *his* spot?

"Yeah. Just to try him out. Now get out there," said Coop.

He's Out!

The teammates threw their gloves on the ground. Gnash angrily whipped his onto the pile. They sprinted out toward the first fence post and each player touched it lightly with one hand. Two of the players ran ahead of everyone else, their long, smooth strides making the drill look easy. Sebastian and Tami brought up the rear, puffing hard.

"This . . ." huffed Sebastian, trying to keep up, ". . . is always the . . . *worst* . . . part . . . of my . . . day!"

"I . . . hear . . . you," puffed Tami.

The coach was standing at second base, watching with a keen eye. "As a group!" Coop shouted to them. "We run as a *team!*"

Jock was well in the lead but he pretended not to hear the coach. He even sped up a little. He touched the second and third fence posts before anyone else and headed back toward the others, who were still on their last pole. When he'd finished, Coop strode over to him.

"You're new so you don't know, but part of the reason we run the poles is to work together as a team," Coop explained. "We play together and we all run together."

Jock shrugged and ran to get his glove.

5 SHORT BENCH

After poles, the coach put the team through fly-ball and grounder drills. But it wasn't a good day for the Blues. Balls were flying everywhere, bouncing randomly and rarely caught. It wasn't long before the team had broken out ice packs and the bench looked like a hospital emergency room. In the dugout, players moaned, iced swollen limbs and compared bruises.

The players who weren't hurt stayed on the field and kept practising.

"Man, I hate the Pirates," Gnash said to Lin, the team's right fielder.

"Yeah, Parkhill sucks," said Lin.

"Money," sneered Gnash, punching his fist in his glove. "Those kids think they're better than us."

"Those stupid white uniforms," said Lin. "They probably get their maids to wash 'em after every game."

"Even their maids probably have maids," said Gnash.

"I heard their water bottles are filled with Perrier," said Lin.

"Yeah. Someone told me they have gourmet pizza at their practices," added Gnash, punching his glove again.

The two turned to look as the Pirates' huge black SUVs began pulling into the parking lot at the top of the hill. Players jumped out and came charging down the hillside toward the Visitor dugout. They hung up their matching baseball bags along its back fence.

Lin and Gnash watched as the Pirates joked with each other while they grabbed their equipment for their warm-up.

Meanwhile, on the other side of the diamond, the Blues' dugout looked like a scene from a zombie movie. There were almost as many parents as players on the bench, mopping at scrapes and applying cold packs.

Coach Coop called the rest of the team in from the field.

"Kids, I'm not gonna lie," he said. "That warm-up hurt us. We've got a short bench now. In fact, I'm going to have to do a head count."

Coop went into the dugout. Gnash watched him approach the moaning players. After Coop had gone down the line, he came back to the infield.

"Jock," he said, "Can you suit up?"

The teammates looked at each other in surprise.

"Coach, we've barely even practised with him," blurted Tami. "We haven't even decided what position he's gonna play!"

"Well, it's not like we have a choice," said Coop. "We're short two players — Jock brings us up to eight, and that's the minimum. So either he plays or we forfeit. What do you guys wanna do?"

The teammates looked toward where the Pirates were warming up. Normally, most of the diamond space at Christie Pits was shaded in the late afternoon. But today, a shaft of golden sunlight was shining right on the Pirates. It made their white uniforms glow.

The Blues turned to look at their own dugout. It was dark and dusty and littered with crushed pop cans and candy wrappers.

"Besides," said the coach, trying to draw the team's attention back to the field, "Jock knows what he's doing. Right, Jock?"

Jock was standing at the back of the pack, and all eyes turned to him.

"Whatever — it doesn't matter to me, I'm fine," he said. And then he added, "Wait, I don't have a jersey."

"You can use your old jersey — it's blue," said Coop. "Just turn it inside-out until we can get you one of ours. Go see one of our parents and they'll get you fixed up."

Jock jogged to the dugout. One of the dads loudly ripped off a piece of grey duct tape and stuck it onto the back of Jock's inside-out shirt. "Now you're number *one*," he told Jock. "It's the easiest number to make out of duct tape."

Coop looked at the rest of the team. "Let's just try and keep it together," he said, in his most encouraging voice. "It's going to be a tough one, but let's just try and get through it — together. Remember, we're a team, no matter what. Stay positive, and let's just get through this."

"On four!" cried Sebastian, jumping to his feet.

All the players stood in a circle and stuck their hands into the centre. "ONE-TWO-THREE, *GO BLUES*!" they shouted, and ran to the dugout. The Blues collected their gear and took one last swig of water before the game.

The coach called out their positions, and everyone waited to hear where Jock would be playing.

"We're going to try Jock out in a couple of different spots," said Coop. "This inning, Jock, try shortstop."

Gnash's face darkened. "What the *he*—" he started to say.

"Just for this inning," said Coop. "You play centre field, Gnash. C'mon, you've got wheels!"

Coop might have been telling Gnash he was fast, but that didn't change the fact that he was replacing him. Gnash headed to the outfield, shooting a fierce look at Jock, who was already in position at shortstop, looking around for a baseball to warm up with.

★★★

By the top of the fifth inning, the score wasn't as bad as the Blues had feared. Even Gnash had to admit that it was mostly because of Jock. Every throw Jock made was hard and accurate. Plus, not a single ball had gotten by him, no matter what position he was playing.

"It's like the kid has a magnet in his glove," said Sebastian after one particularly awe-inspiring catch.

"Yeah, and the ball is made of metal," added the other team's coach, with a smile that didn't hide his envy. "Got to hand it to you guys. I don't know how you got him, but that kid's amazing."

"We pay him a lot," Sebastian joked. "Of course, it's in *sunflower seeds*, but still."

The other team's coach chuckled and returned to his own dugout.

The score was 7–6 for the Pirates, and Coop called out to Jock to switch to centre field. "Gnash, come back in to short," he yelled.

As the boys passed each other, Gnash glared at Jock. "Thanks for keeping my spot warm," he said.

"Yeah, no problem," said Jock. "Just make sure it stays that way. Then maybe we've got a chance against these guys, eh? 'Course, that would mean you'd have to actually *hit a ball* this inning. Think you could try that?"

While Gnash had struck out three times so far, Jock had been responsible for four of the Blues' six runs. He'd belted two homers and hit two scoring doubles that the Pirates' outfielders couldn't even touch.

Gnash growled and turned away, his face red, as he struggled to think of a comeback.

The boys took their positions as a short girl with a half-shaved haircut stepped into the box. She was a heavy hitter and one of the strongest players in the league.

"Back up, everyone," Coop yelled to his outfielders.

The batter planted her feet and squinted at Raj on the mound. She raised her bat and, as the ball came in, cracked it with all of her might. The sound of the ball hitting the aluminum bat echoed across the Pits. The soccer players two fields over turned to look for the source of the sound.

The girl took off toward first as the ball sailed toward centre field. It was going so fast it seemed to pick up speed the higher it went. She touched first and was rounding second before the ball had even begun its descent.

"I've got it! I've got it!" yelled Gnash, waving off Jock.

"You don't 'got it,'" said Jock, watching as Gnash zig-zagged around, trying to position himself underneath the ball. It soared up and up until it was nearly lost in the pale blue sky.

"Get back," Jock directed Gnash. "You need to get back a lot farther!"

"I've *got* it!" cried Gnash again, wildly waving his arm to push Jock away. The other players watched to see whether Gnash would be able to catch the ball. But by the time Gnash's brain told him that he needed to run farther back and Gnash's legs agreed to do the job, it was too late. His momentum was pushing him forward but the ball was arcing backward. The ball headed toward a spot twenty-five feet past where Gnash was weaving. He was left lurching, open-mouthed and red-faced, with his glove up in the air. As the ball floated past him, Gnash's expression changed from surprise to disappointment. And then it turned to anger when he spotted Jock, perfectly positioned in the ball's landing spot.

"I told you that you weren't going back far enough," Jock said over his shoulder, as he easily caught the ball. In the same motion, he brought his other hand up to his glove, plucked the ball out and threw it straight to Raj on the mound. There was a loud snap as it landed in the pitcher's glove.

"Yerrrrrr *out!*" said the umpire, as the batter skidded to a stop near third base. She looked stunned that her huge bomb had been caught.

As she walked back to her dugout, cheers and applause for Jock's catch burst from the Blues' bench. However, the voices died down as the Blues began to pick up on Gnash's anger.

Soon, the crunch of shoes on the dry infield dirt and far-off curses and laughter from the soccer players were the only sounds in the Pits.

Coop took off his baseball cap and ran his fingers through his sweaty faux-hawk. Then he tamped the cap back down onto his head.

In a sudden outburst, Gnash angrily threw his glove onto the ground. He wound up his foot and gave the glove a kick that sent it flying toward third base.

"Seriously?" asked Jock. And then he added in a squeaky sing-song taunt, "and is *that* how we treat our equipment?"

"Shut up!" yelled Gnash, his face beet red. "Shut up! Shut *up!*"

Gnash launched himself toward the taller boy, charging at him with his head down like an angry goat. Jock was caught off-guard by the attack. Soon he was on his back with his glove over his face, covered by Gnash who was landing blows anywhere he could find a soft spot.

The dugout cleared as the entire team ran to pull the boys apart. Each player grabbed a limb or a piece of jersey and yelled at the two to stop fighting.

It was a long time before the players' voices lost their frantic edge, but eventually the scene faded into two camps. Each clump of kids held one of the combatants at its centre.

Jock was doubled over with his arms wrapped around his stomach. "I think you broke a rib, you stupid orangutan!" he shouted at Gnash.

Gnash, blotchy-faced and puffing, hadn't given up.

He flailed his arms, desperately trying to reach Jock.

"Yeah, well, at least I'm not . . . I'm not . . . *gay!*" he yelled through the tangle of teammates holding him back. "Yeah, *that's* right," he said. "You're totally *gay!*" He looked triumphantly around at his teammates.

Jock's head was down and his shoulders began to shake. Raj put his arm protectively around the boy's shoulders.

"C'mon, leave him alone," Raj said to Gnash.

Jock's shoulders shook more heavily and, still doubled over, he began to blubber.

"Wait . . . *wait* . . ." he huffed, between spasms, "that's . . ."

Jock stood up. He was laughing!

"That's . . ." he sputtered, "that's the best you can do? 'You're *gay'*?" Jock took a deep breath. "Uh, yeah, and you're . . . Italian! You moron, I know I'm gay. *Everyone* knows I'm gay. When I made all-star, the newspaper wrote an article that said I'm gay! It's not a secret. And by the way, it's the twenty-first century — *gay* is not an insult. It's the way I was born." Jock was still laughing, but it didn't quite reach his eyes. They glinted with anger.

"On the other hand," he added, his smile fading, "how'd you become such a *loser*? Were you born that way — or do you have to work at it?"

Gnash stopped fighting the kids holding him back. He stared at Jock. Gnash knew he'd just been insulted, but he couldn't quite put his finger on how.

"Wow," said Jock, looking around at the team. "Just . . . wow. You guys are even lamer than I thought you were."

Jock roughly shook the players' hands off him and broke through the circle. He walked toward left field, the way he and Coop had first come to the ball diamond. As he passed Coop, he hissed, "I *told* you this would happen."

Coop watched Jock walk away. Then he strode to home plate. Through clenched teeth he said to the umpire, "We forfeit."

6 COOP'S BREAK-UP

At school the next day, Raj and Gnash leaned against the wall near French class. They watched Sebastian frantically searching through the rubble of school supplies and books in his locker.

"It was here before, I know it was," said Sebastian. "I've got to find it! Ah . . . *voila*!" he said, triumphantly, holding his French textbook in the air.

"I've never seen Coop so angry," said Raj.

"I know," said Sebastian, tucking the book under his arm. He began rifling through his locker for his binder. "How long were we at the diamond last night?"

"I think Coop stopped yelling around . . . maybe 8:15?"

"Naw, it had to be later than that," said Gnash. "The streetlights had been on for, like, an hour."

"He was *apoplectic*," said Raj.

"He sure was," said Sebastian. "Assuming that means 'angry.'"

"It does," said Raj. "Really angry."

Gnash looked grim. "Yeah, well, I don't know what he was steamed about," he said. "That . . . *American* guy . . . started it!"

Raj grabbed Sebastian's French binder from the top shelf of his locker and passed it to him. "But we deserved everything Coop dished out," Raj said.

"No. I agree with Gnash," said Sebastian. "It didn't make any sense. What did we do? Tried to save two kids from beating each other to death? Tried to win against those lousy rich snobs? Coop was totally out of line, yelling at us like that."

Gnash nodded.

"Hmm," said Raj. "Do you think maybe you guys missed the point of Coop's lecture last night?"

"Actually, I've been thinking about it," said Sebastian, wrinkling his forehead. "I figured maybe Coop broke up with his girlfriend. Don't you think that would make him pretty angry? But that's not *our* fault!"

Tami and Lin joined them. "Has anyone seen Jock today?" Tami asked.

"Nope," said Raj. "And I wouldn't blame him if he didn't come to school today."

"Me either," said Tami. "I feel sick about what happened."

"Why, you heard about Coop's girlfriend?" asked Sebastian.

Tami turned to the catcher. "Coop's girlfriend?" she asked.

"Yeah," said Raj with a laugh. "Apparently that's why Coop was so mad last night — at least, according to Sebastian. He must have broken up with his girlfriend."

"Oh, right," said Lin. "It probably had *nothing* to do with us outing a guy and telling everyone he's gay. Or talking about him behind his back. Or starting a fist fight at centre field." She looked pointedly at Gnash.

Gnash turned away.

"Yeah, or possibly making us lose one of the best players we've ever had," added Raj.

Sebastian scratched his head. "Hey, are you guys being sarcastic?" he asked.

"*Yes*, Sebastian! Yes, we are!" Tami said, exasperated. "Sometimes you can be totally dense!"

"But you've got to give Jock credit," said Lin. "That was a pretty awesome response, eh? He basically told you where to go, Gnash!"

Gnash stiffened as Raj laughed and said, "Yeah, remember when we all thought he was crying his head off?"

"And then he comes up laughing?" said Tami. "That was classic!"

"I have to go to class," grumbled Gnash, pushing himself off from the wall.

"I guess they're more casual in New Jersey about being gay," said Sebastian. "I mean, being gay's not a good thing, right? Right?"

"Holy cow, Sebastian, what's the matter with you?" Tami laughed and shoved Sebastian in the direction Gnash was walking.

"Just go to class!" she and Lin said, almost in unison.

"Listen, Sebastian," Raj called after him. "We want Jock on our team and that's all you need to know."

Sebastian stopped and nodded his head slowly. "Yeah. We did nearly win that game because of him. He was amazing."

★★★

The first day back on the field for the Blues after the dust-up between Gnash and Jock was the following Sunday. Coop had called a practice before their game against the Etobicoke Reds.

One of the boys nodded hello to Gnash as he stormed by them to hang his bag on the back fence of the dugout. He ignored the greeting and sifted through his bag for his glove.

Coop called the players out onto the field.

"I want you guys to run some poles and then line up for throwing," he said in a quiet voice — at least, quiet for Coop. "Go."

The players looked at each other. "Coop," said Sebastian, "Uh ..."

"What?" asked Coop grimly.

"Uh ... uh ..." And then Sebastian brightened.

"How's your weekend been going so far, man?"

Coop stared at Sebastian in disbelief. The players held their breath.

Coop took one look at Sebastian's broad, cheesy grin and burst out laughing.

"Get out there, you guys — go do your poles!" he barked with a grin. Everyone ran toward the outfield.

Most of the team jogged off. Raj stayed behind, pulling Coop and Gnash aside.

"Listen," he said. "What do you think the chances are that Jock will come back to the team?"

"I talked to him yesterday," said Coop, "and I talked to his mom. It wasn't good. They were both pretty upset. Apparently he's been getting messed around at school by some kids. And the way we were treating him on top of that . . . he basically told me that he doesn't want to be on a team where he doesn't feel welcome."

"Yeah, I saw some of that at school," said Raj. "Did he tell you who's been pushing him around?"

"No," said Coop. "Does it really matter, though? I mean, this kid is an amazing athlete and look at all the crap he has to put up with!"

"Yeah, it sucks," said Raj.

"Humph," Gnash grunted. He snatched his batting gloves from the dugout floor and shoved them into his back pocket.

"Anyway, I did my best," said Coop. "I told him and his mom that I had talked to the team. But I'm not sure that everyone fully understands what the problem is, do you?"

"Maybe some of the kids just need to know Jock a bit better," said Raj, looking off at the horizon around the field. "I think Jock's a pretty good guy — even if he maybe isn't the easiest guy to get along with. And he's, like, crazy good at baseball."

Gnash's face darkened.

"Well, that's the other thing," said Coop. "Back home, this kid wasn't just an all-star, he was his league's MVP. We're lucky that he moved to Toronto and that he wants to play with us. But all of that means nothing if our team can't get along. I mean, I know you guys are just kids and all, but geez . . . the bunch of you need to grow up, eh?" He smiled a little and Raj stepped out to join in running the poles.

Raj turned around. "So do you think he'll come back?" he asked.

Gnash brushed by him on his way out to the field.

"I sure hope so," said Coop. "Our guys aren't bad kids, just maybe a bit . . . uninformed. I still think we can work it out."

"At least," he added, "I sure hope so."

7 SECOND CHANCE

The Blues needed a win, and not just for their standings in the league — the Blues were locked in a friendly, long-standing rivalry with Etobicoke.

"And the rivalry continues!" said Sebastian with a loud, dramatic flourish.

"Yep," said Miguel. "I'm sick of tying these guys!"

"Hey, the difference between a tie and a win is one run," said Coop. "Just one. So c'mon! Let's go!"

"Yeah," called Sebastian, taking up the charge. "Three up, three down!"

That did it. Instantly, there was an answering chorus of "Three up, three down!" and "Who is fired up? We are fired up!" The din coming from the Blues' bench echoed across the Pits.

"Okay, okay, guys, now let's focus on the game," said Coop. "Here's what I want you to remember out there. Ready positions — I don't want to see anyone lazing around in the outfield. As soon as that batter walks out there, you should be in your ready position. Got that?"

There were murmurs of agreement from the players.

"And don't forget to shift. If it's a right-handed batter, where do we go?"

"Righty-shift!" yelled the players together.

"Exactly. Watch me for the signs, but you should be shifting before I even have to tell you," said Coop. "I wanna hear you talking out there, kids. Communicate. Now, hands in!"

The players each put one hand into the middle and Tami yelled, "*ONE-TWO-THREE-BLUES!*" The teammates cheered and ran out to take their positions.

By the top of the fourth inning the teams were in a dead heat. The Blues were playing as well as they could, but Gnash knew they were making too many errors.

"If we had Jock in the field last inning we'd be ahead by three runs," said Tami to Lin as they sat waiting to bat. "They had two guys in scoring position and we missed that fly ball."

"Yeah," agreed Lin, in a low voice. "She'd have been out and we'd be ahead because Jock would have caught that one. Actually, we could use him in the line-up, too — right now. We need a run."

At the end of the bench, Gnash scowled. He was still having trouble figuring out where to move for fly balls. More than once, balls that he should have caught had gotten by him. He thought about Jock telling him to get back farther and, although he didn't like to admit it, it was a good strategy. But it was hard, when the ball was coming high and fast and every eye was on him. His glove seemed to shrink to an impossibly small size and the ball got lost against the clouds. Sometimes he could swear it seemed to change direction before it got to him.

Gnash was even more tense as he took his place in the on-deck circle. His eyebrows knitted together as he watched the Reds' pitcher throw his warm-up pitches. As each pitch went over the plate, Gnash took a hard practice swing, timing it as if he was at the plate.

By the time he heard the Reds' catcher cry "second base, coming down!" Gnash was ready. He looked over at Coop, who gave him the sign for *take*. He shook his head at the coach. Coop gave him the take sign again, this time with more energy. Gnash shook his head again and then turned away to step into the batter's box.

What was Coop thinking? He couldn't just let the first pitch go by without at least trying to hit it.

When the ball came toward Gnash, it looked to him like low-hanging fruit. He swung. But the ball was lower than he thought, and outside. Although he made a solid cut, the ball loped high into the air over the right fielder, who caught it easily.

"Catch!" yelled the ump.

★★★

Two days later, the team was back at the Pits to warm up before another game against the Reds.

It wasn't until the team was on their fourth pole that Gnash glanced up the steep hill to the sidewalk, where he saw the coach talking to Jock. A tall, elegant-looking woman, who Gnash guessed was Jock's mother, was with them.

"Hey." Gnash nudged Raj and Tami, as the three of them jogged at the back of the pack. "Check that out."

Raj craned his neck to see where Gnash was pointing.

"That doesn't look too good," said Tami.

"No, it's good, it's good," said Raj, between strides. "If Jock wasn't coming back to the team, he wouldn't have come here, would he?"

"I guess not," puffed Tami. She snorted and launched a mouthful of spit onto the ground beside them. "Yeah, you're right, actually. He would have just never showed up again."

By now, all of the teammates had noticed the conference taking place at the top of the hill. They slowed down to a walk. All heads turned to the scene. No one said a word.

Finally, Gnash said, "Huh. What a loser."

Raj had had enough. "Gnash!" he said, exasperated.

"What?" said Gnash gruffly. "You taking his side now? The guy's a jerk!"

"Well, he's an all-star jerk, then," said Raj. "He's an MVP jerk. He's the kind of jerk this team could use!" Raj threw his hands up in the air and said, "Why do we have to take sides, Gnash? What's your problem with him, anyway? You don't even know this guy. You know absolutely nothing about him. Nothing!"

"I know that he's *gay*," sneered Gnash.

"Keep talking, Gnash. Keep saying that word. Maybe one day it won't sound like an insult coming out of your mouth." Raj began to walk away. Then he turned back suddenly. "Look, you guys, I know that Jock's maybe not the friendliest guy we've ever met. But don't you think we should at least give him a fair shot? If for no other reason than he's probably the best player we've ever seen . . . maybe the best player this league has ever seen . . . and he's willing to play for us?"

"Well, wait," said Sebastian, scratching his head under his baseball cap. Sweat streamed down his face. "If he wants to play for us . . . doesn't that just show that this guy has, like, poor judgment?"

Everyone on the team turned and stared at Sebastian in silence. Sebastian blinked.

And then Raj burst out laughing. Gnash stopped walking and started laughing, too, dropping his forehead onto his palm. The entire team was soon in stitches over Sebastian's take on the situation. Sebastian looked around at his teammates, his face confused. Then he joined in, too.

Still chuckling, Raj began sprinting up the hill. "Oh man," he laughed. "Sebastian!"

Gnash watched Raj dash up the hill until he reached

Jock. Coop and Jock's mother were a few metres away, talking together.

Gnash couldn't hear what Raj was saying to Jock up on the sidewalk. He supposed the pitcher was trying to persuade Jock to rejoin the team.

Gnash was just about to turn away, when he saw Jock grab Raj's arm. Gnash watched as Jock pulled Raj toward him and suddenly, the American was kicking Raj's foot.

"What the—?" muttered Gnash, watching the strange scene. "Hey, guys," he said, motioning for them to come over. "I think that new kid is attacking Raj!"

8 FOOLED ON THE HILL

The rest of the Blues watched in disbelief as Jock pulled Raj close and held one of his arms behind his back.

"Oh my god, he's putting the moves on him!" said Sebastian, his voice becoming shrill with fear.

"We've got to do something," said Lin, coming up behind Gnash and Sebastian.

But Gnash was already headed up the hill as fast as he could go. He charged toward his best friend and the attacker. As he struggled up the steep incline, he called out to Jock, "Hey, freak! Get away from him!"

Sebastian followed closely behind Gnash, with the rest of the team on their tails. They climbed the slope as fast as they could, slipping on the tall weeds and loose dirt as they fought to get to the top.

Gnash was the first to reach the two boys.

"Hey! Get off him!" Gnash panted. He grabbed Jock's hand and roughly tore it away from Raj's arm.

Jock's mother and Coop ran over to where the boys were yelling.

"Hey, hey, what's going on here?" asked Coop, holding on to the back of Gnash's jersey.

"He's attacking Raj!" Sebastian said, pointing at Jock. The rest of the teammates chimed in, backing up Sebastian and trying to make Coop see how dangerous the situation was.

"Hold on, hold on," said Raj, holding up his hands. "He was just giving me a couple of pointers!"

"He was giving him *pointers*, too!" said Sebastian, his eyes wide with alarm.

"Pointers, Sebastian — you know, pitching advice."

"Huh?" said Sebastian. He was still puffing from the exertion of his jog up the hill.

"You idiots are way outta line," said Raj. "He was helping me with my pitching stance. Look!"

Raj held a ball in one of his hands and shifted his front foot. "Jock was saying that whenever I take my stride, my front foot sticks out toward the third-base line. He said it needs to be pointing toward the plate more."

Jock came over and kicked Raj's front toe over, straighter.

"Like that," said Jock.

"See?" said Raj.

Jock looked over at the group of Blues and smiled.

"What's your problem?" asked Gnash. "Is something funny?"

"Oh, come on, Gnash. It's *funny*!" said Jock. "You

thought I was trying to . . . what? Come on to Raj? Sebastian — you actually thought I would attack him?"

"Well, from down there, it looked like you had him in a hug or something," grumbled Gnash, a little uncertainly. "And we definitely saw you kick him. You can't deny that you kicked him!"

"Yeah, and I just did it again right in front of you, you jerks," said Jock. "Look, I'm not evil and I'm sure not hitting on Raj. And, before you accuse me of it, I'm also not trying to hit on *you* — trust me, you're not my type. So can we just get past all this crap and play some frigging baseball?"

"Oh, man," said Raj. "I had just convinced him to play for us again when you morons came up here. We're lucky that he thinks this is funny."

"Yeah, and that he doesn't sue us," said Sebastian. "My dad says Americans will sue at the drop of a — *hey!*"

Tami shoved Sebastian so hard his legs flew out from under him.

"What did you do that for?" he said, scrambling awkwardly to his feet.

"Let's just say it was . . . pre-emptive," said Tami.

"Well, I should *sue* you!" said Sebastian.

Gnash saw Jock and his mother talking together. She finally nodded and gave her son a quick hug.

Coop took out his cell phone and glanced at the time. "Look, we still have forty minutes before the game. C'mon, guys," he said. "Let's get back down there and finish our warm-up."

Most of the Blues turned and began to sprint back down the hill.

Jock walked over to Raj and Gnash and the three of them made their way down the hill together.

"Listen, Jock," said Raj as they trudged down the incline toward the field.

"Yeah?" asked Jock.

"I wonder if you could do something for me," said Raj.

"What's that?" asked Jock, instantly wary.

"Maybe you could give the guys a bit of a break?"

"What? *Me* give *them* a break?"

"Yeah," said Raj.

"What, like, you want me to suck up to them?" asked Jock, his eyes widening.

"Well, no, not suck up," said Raj.

"Make nice," said Jock, pursing his lips together.

"Yeah, I guess so," said Raj.

"They've kind of been jerky to me, you know," said Jock, looking at Gnash. Gnash kept his head down, his eyes shielded underneath his baseball cap.

"I know," agreed Raj. "Even so."

"Even so."

"Thanks," said Raj.

9 SEEING RED

Forty minutes later, the team was in place on the field. It was the top of the first inning in the second game against the Reds. Raj was standing on the pitcher's mound. He was about to pitch against his second batter. Gnash watched him step off the rubber to dust his hands with the white mesh chalk bag next to the mound. He clapped it between his hands, creating a puffy white cloud.

Raj settled back on his heels and took a look around. The first Reds batter had made it to second and was threatening to take third.

Raj ignored him and grimly stepped back onto the mound. He twisted the toes of his right shoe back and forth, digging it into the dirt next to the rubber. "Toward the plate," Gnash heard him say. "Left foot points toward the plate."

The batter was a lanky boy Gnash knew well. He was the kind of kid who could make it to first before anyone, even Jock, would be able to stop him.

Gnash waited to see what kind of pitch Raj would choose. If the kid even got a piece of it, there'd be a man on first.

Sebastian was squatting over the plate with his glove held up facing Raj. He flashed the signal for an inside fastball.

"*Just hit the target,*" Raj muttered, and he wound up. "*Left foot straight . . . FOR-ward!*" He launched the ball toward the batter, fast and hard and perfectly over the plate just on the inside. The batter swung lamely, well after the ball had already passed him.

"Steeeeee-rike!" the umpire called, pumping his fist.

It wasn't until the second pitch had left Raj's hand that Gnash noticed Raj hadn't positioned his front foot. It was pointing the wrong way. The ball didn't go where it was supposed to. Another wounded soldier took a base, rubbing his thigh muscle where the ball had hit him.

Now there was a man on third and a man on first.

Raj stepped off again.

No one was surprised when Coop called a time-out and headed out to speak with Raj. But the team *was* surprised when Jock came jogging in to join the conversation. Jock got to Raj before Coop did and Gnash and the other infielders joined them on the mound.

"Don't worry about it so much, Raj," said Jock.

"What do you mean?" asked Raj.

"Hitting the batter. Don't worry about it so much. Everyone knows you're not hitting the batter on purpose. And anyway, hitting that last guy wasn't a bad idea — if he'd gotten a piece of the ball, it would've gone out to centre field *at least*. Anyway, just focus on the target, remember your feet and relax."

"Thanks, Jock — ahem," said Coop, interrupting. "I can handle it from here, if you don't mind. Everyone, go back to your spots." No one listened to the coach and the mound remained piled with Blues. Even some of the outfielders came in to listen to the conversation.

"It's true, though, Raj," said Coop. "Listen, you have one of the lowest Earned Run Averages our team has ever seen. You're a good pitcher, we all know that."

The players on the mound nodded in support.

"You don't have to prove anything, and you sure as heck don't have to worry about nailing someone like that guy. Anyway, he was crowding the plate. Just do what you're here to do. Do what you do," said Coop.

"And watch your front foot!" Jock called over.

The coach headed back to his spot by the dugout.

Raj scowled and climbed the dirt. He turned and looked over at the kid on first and the boy who was now on third. It was obvious Raj wanted to get out of the inning without hitting anyone else. And he wanted his infield to get that kid on third out so he didn't score.

Raj looked carefully down at his front foot. He took a deep breath and went into his wind-up. The fastball left his fingertips and everyone knew that it would go right where the batter didn't want it to be. After the throw, Raj looked down at his feet again. Sure enough, his front foot was pointed straight toward the plate.

Before his next pitch, and the one after that, Raj made a point of looking down at his feet.

The boy on third never got a chance to leave his base, because Raj struck the next two batters out.

The top of the inning ended and everyone ran in. Raj's teammates punched him on the shoulder and slapped his back.

"That was great!" cheered Sebastian. "And I really liked that dance-thing you were doing on the mound."

"What dance-thing?" asked Raj.

"That thing where you kept shifting your feet. The Twist."

Raj looked over at Tami and Jock. As they made eye contact, all three of them burst out laughing.

Gnash was on the other side of the dugout. Under hooded eyelids, he watched the exchange between his teammates. Even Gnash had to admit that the advice Jock had given Raj seemed to be working. But he didn't see why Raj had to be so chummy with the new kid.

The game with the Reds ended in a 5–5 tie. It wasn't the outcome the Blues had been hoping for, but at least it wasn't a loss. And the infield had kept the number of runs down to single digits, which didn't always happen.

All but one of the runs for the Blues had been due to Jock. He had gotten an inside-the-park home run and three runs batted in.

"I might be able to bring my Earned Run Average down before the end of the season," Raj said to Jock. "Hey, maybe there's hope for me yet!"

Gnash looked away.

"Maybe," he told his friend. But he wasn't so sure.

10 MUDBALL

When Gnash woke up the next morning it was pouring rain. He looked at his phone and saw that the weather forecast was calling for heavy rain for the whole day.

"Where do you think you're going?" Gnash's grandfather asked him as he headed out the door, his baseball bag slung over one shoulder.

Gnash lived with his grandparents, and he couldn't recall the last time his grandfather had said anything nice to him — unless Gnash hit a home run. Then his grandfather was all smiles and all, "That's *my* boy!" Gnash had only hit two home runs since he'd started playing baseball. It was a long time to wait between pats on the back.

Gnash stopped in his tracks. He looked down. "To the Pits," he said quietly.

"Nice. Gonna go practice with your new *boyfriends*?" his grandfather sneered.

Gnash tried to sidle past his grandfather. But, although he was much older, the man was still imposing.

His grandfather stopped him by putting a hand on his shoulder.

"Are you gonna play baseball . . . or something *else* with your *pals*?" He smirked.

Gnash was never sure if he was meant to laugh along with his grandfather's mean jokes.

"Baseball," he mumbled, and made another attempt to get by.

"*Naaa-aaash*," his grandmother called from the kitchen.

"Yeah, Gramma?" Gnash moved away from his grandfather and ducked into the small kitchen.

His grandmother was a petite woman. Her back was hunched from years of washing dishes at the small apartment's low sink. "It's raining out. Are you going to be warm enough?" She held a cereal bowl in one hand and a dish towel in the other.

Gnash walked over to the tiny woman and hugged her. He kissed the top of her wiry, grey top-knot. "I'll be fine, Gramma, thanks. If it rains any harder, I'll come home."

He tucked a stray wisp of grey hair behind her ear and she smiled at him. "Say something nice to your grandfather," she said. "He worries about you."

"I know he does, Gramma," said Gnash, giving her a squeeze.

Fortunately, his grandfather was nowhere to be seen as Gnash left the apartment. He took the stairs two at a time down to the rainy sidewalk.

Even if the rain stopped before the afternoon, Gnash knew, there would be no way the team could practice. The diamonds at Christie Pits were notorious for flooding. The water would collect on the infield and form puddles that no amount of sand could soak up. At the Pits, rainouts were a regular occurrence.

Even so, by the time Gnash reached the park, most of the team was huddled around Jock. He was smiling and laughing in the streaming rain.

"And whoever's left standing is up next," Jock was saying.

"Wait, wait, what are we talking about?" interrupted Gnash as he reached them.

"Mudball!" said Sebastian, his face framed by rain-soaked tendrils of hair. "Jock's teaching us how to play."

"Gee, that sounds like a fun baby-game," said Gnash. The rain was drizzling uncomfortably down his back.

"We used to play it whenever we got rained out back home," said Jock. "Christie Pits is perfect for it — I wish we'd had these hills in New Jersey."

"Yeah, well, it sounds stupid to me," said Gnash, wiping the rain out of his eyes. "I'm going home. You losers can play your little game. Have fun!"

Not even Raj glanced at Gnash as he headed up the hill.

Gnash couldn't believe how quickly his stupid friends had turned on him. He used to be the one who decided what the team would do on off-days. Now they were listening to the American kid — the gay kid.

But Gnash didn't want to go home, either. He walked over to a large oak tree beside the sidewalk at the top of the hill and sat, propping his back against the trunk.

Gnash watched his friends through the curtain of cold rain as Jock repeated the rules.

"So," he said. "One kid's *it* — he's the mudball. The other kids take up a spot on the hill. The kid who's *it* yells 'mudball!' and everyone has to freeze where they are. They're not allowed to move, except to jump up. The mudball guy rolls down the hill and he tries to knock over as many kids as he can. For every kid he knocks down, he gets a point. That's it. Most points wins."

"Yeah, and a fall-down counts as a knock-down," said Lin.

"Okay, got it," said Raj. "Who's the first mudball?"

Everyone on the team quickly shouted "Not it!" almost in unison.

Jock, who didn't know about the "called-it" rule, was the only who hadn't shouted "not it."

"You're it!" shouted Lin, pointing to him.

Jock held his hands up. "All right, I'm the mudball," he said and he ran up the hill, slipping on patches of wet muck as he went. He stopped close to where Gnash was sitting.

Gnash assumed Jock was coming over to talk him into playing. He started to invent a reason why he wasn't going to join them when Jock suddenly yelled "*Mudball!*"

"Hey, no fair!" said Sebastian, who was right in front of Jock near the hilltop. "I wasn't ready!"

"Ha! I know!" said Jock, smiling. "*Geronimoooooo!*" And he flopped onto his side and rolled straight into Sebastian, knocking him off his feet. The two boys rolled around until Sebastian untangled himself. He sat down in a river of rainwater that was streaming down the hillside.

Jock wiped some mud away from his eyes. He looked around for his next target. He spotted Lin and Tami, who weren't looking his way. He angled himself to plow into the girls. He rolled and caught Tami completely unawares. Lin leapt up, but Jock rolled backward so he was underneath her feet as she came down. Lin landed heavily on Jock, who gave another half-roll to shake her off onto the ground.

"Ha! That's three!" he said happily, looking around for his next victim.

By the time he'd zig-zagged to the bottom of the hill, Jock had successfully taken down every one of the six teammates. They began picking up handfuls of mud and flinging them at Jock and each other.

"I've got six points!" said Jock. He laughed and rubbed his right knee where he'd knocked it against a rock when he'd taken out Raj. "Who's *it*?"

"I wanna be the mudball!" said Sebastian, sticking his hand up in the air and jumping around. "I'm *it*! I'm *it*!"

The game went on for two more hours, long after the rain had stopped. By the time the players realized they were thirsty and starving, they were so caked in mud they were nearly unrecognizable. Bone-tired and filthy but happy, they clawed their way up the slippery slope and headed home.

No one noticed Gnash trudging toward the bus stop.

11 DOING THE MATH

The next day was Monday and Gnash sat in Math class trying not to think about the detentions he had earned the previous week.

If someone did something wrong and Gnash was nearby, teachers just assumed it was him. If there was a smell or a spill or a mess in the classroom, the first person any teacher blamed was Gnash. If Gnash didn't have an alibi, he was automatically guilty. Only about six times out of ten was it actually true. But Gnash wasn't a snitch and he'd rather serve someone else's detention than give someone up to the teacher.

So, when a pencil was launched across the room while the teacher was at the blackboard with her back turned, she immediately turned on Gnash. Gnash steeled himself for what was coming — another unfair detention. He was surprised when Jock got up from his seat.

"Sorry, Ms. Euclid. My bad!" Jock said with a cheerful grin.

Jock jogged over to retrieve the pencil, as though running around Math class and sassing the teacher was what every kid did, and got away with.

The teacher looked at Jock, and then over at Gnash, who was staring straight ahead at nothing.

"Sit down, Mr. Christobel," said Ms. Euclid. "We don't jog around the classroom. This isn't Gym class."

"I was just playing with my pencil and it sort of — flew out of my hand," said Jock.

"That's fine, that's fine," said Ms. Euclid. "Just please retrieve it and sit down."

Jock looked over at Gnash, who was struggling to keep his face neutral. If he'd ever tried to pull a stunt that cheeky he would have had detention for a week! Eventually Gnash looked over at Jock — this time, at least, he wasn't going to get the blame.

Jock winked at him, turning so the teacher couldn't see them.

"Freak," Gnash said under his breath.

As Jock walked by Gnash, he laid his Math textbook quietly down on Gnash's desk and grabbed Gnash's book.

Gnash could see a piece of paper sticking out of the textbook Jock had put in front of him. Before the teacher could spot it, Gnash quickly covered it with his hands. He might not like Jock, but he knew the rules for note-passing and rule number one was, "Always hide the note from the teacher."

Doing the Math

Gnash glared at Jock, whose chair was now noisily scraping the floor and clanking against his desk as he sat down. Jock's eyes were smiling — he seemed to be enjoying himself.

When the ruckus died down, the teacher turned back to the board to write out the day's Geometry lesson.

Gnash quietly slid the folded piece of paper out from the book's pages. On the front flap, in Jock's handwriting, it said, "Gnash is a loser." Gnash felt his face heat up. Silently, he opened the note so he could read what was written inside.

"Now that I have your attention," the note read, "here's some advice. When you're fielding, always go back *first*. Farther than you think. Then if you have to run forward, you can. Pg. 118."

Gnash rifled through the pages until he came to 118. It was a lesson about arcs, and Gnash saw that someone had drawn lines on top of a diagram in the book. At the topmost point of the arc was a hand-drawn baseball, with a dotted pencil line straight down to two shaky stick figures. Gnash guessed they were baseball players from the fat, cartoon gloves at the ends of their stick-arms. The diagram showed one player farther back than the other. It was clear by the angle of the arc that that was the player who was in the right position to catch the ball.

Gnash was still studying the diagram when the bell

rang to signal the end of class. Suddenly, Jock was over at Gnash's desk and his finger was on the diagram.

"See, this is the point where you should make your decision about where to run," said Jock, sliding his finger along the top of the arc. "Run back, so you're here. And then wait until the ball is here. Then, you can either stay where you are and catch the ball, or you can run forward if you have to. But at least you'll be in a better position to see it and to catch it."

Gnash looked away. There was no way he was going to let Jock see he was interested in the discussion.

"What would I do without you?" Gnash sneered. "Can I have my Math book back, please, *Coach*? This one's been vandalized — some annoying person has scribbled in it."

Jock's cheerful smile faded and he handed Gnash back his textbook. Gnash pushed past Jock to the door. On his way out, he loudly dropped Jock's textbook onto his desk.

Jock watched Gnash leave the room. He shook his head and then went over to his own desk. He picked up his textbook and opened it. Page 118 was missing.

In the hallway, Gnash carefully folded the page he had ripped out of Jock's book into a neat square. He put page 118 deep inside his back pocket so it wouldn't fall out.

★★★

Doing the Math

That evening after dinner, Gnash headed down to Christie Pits. He needed to work off some of the confusion and anger he felt after Jock's stunt in Math class. It was bad enough when people were mean to him — but for some reason it was so much worse when people tried to be nice. He wasn't used to people helping him. He knew they were just feeling sorry for him, and that made him feel weak. Gnash didn't like feeling weak.

So he was gnashing his teeth as he walked along the sidewalk, his baseball bag slung over his shoulder. It bumped against his leg with every step. He headed down the steep hill into the Pits.

It was one of the rare days when the Blues' diamond wasn't being used. It was starting to get dark, but teams were practising on the other ball diamonds and on the soccer fields, so the park lights were blazing. Gnash hung his bag on the fence and rummaged around in it until he found his bat and glove. He shoved his cap tightly onto his head. He was wearing his old, ripped baseball pants. He extracted a neatly folded square of paper from one of the shallow back pockets. He left the dugout and unfolded the page. He poked the corners through the holes in the fence so that the diagram of an arc and two baseball players was visible to him from the infield.

Then, taking a handful of scuffed baseballs from his bag, Gnash walked to home plate. He stood underneath the curved fence, looking out at the field. As he looked from base to base, squinting to block out the harsh diamond lights, he imagined the rest of his team. Raj on the mound, Tami at third and Miguel on first. He thought about where he would be standing at short-stop. He looked at the diagram again, and then back to where he pictured himself on the infield.

He tossed a baseball straight up and swung at it with the aluminum bat, as hard as he could. He heard the metallic crack and watched the ball sail up into the air. It was about seven feet high as it blasted over the short-stop position. It continued to rise for another foot or so and Gnash tried to take note of its highest point before it started to arc downward. He picked up another base-ball and hit it as hard as he could. He watched it care-fully and noted where it lost altitude. Then, not taking his eyes from that point on the field, he ran out until he was standing on the spot. He felt around in his pockets and pulled out an empty Snickers wrapper, which he dropped on the ground to mark the location.

Gnash ran back to home plate and hit three more balls to the outfield, watching to see if his Snickers wrapper was at the spot where they started to fall back to Earth. He jogged over to the diagram and snatched it off the fence. He compared it to the real-life positions, thinking about how far back a shortstop would have to run to catch the fly balls.

He was deep in thought, still squinting at the dia-gram, when he heard the rough scratch of cleats on dirt.

He looked up to find Jock striding toward him. "Great," Gnash muttered as he crumpled up the diagram and shoved it hastily into his pocket.

"What are you doing here?" Gnash asked roughly.

Jock smiled half-heartedly. "Just wanted to get in a bit of extra practice," he said. "You?"

"Same," said Gnash, picking up the balls that were scattered around the outfield.

"So, let's hit to each other, then," said Jock.

It was an unwritten rule in sports that you didn't have to be friends to play together. In fact, the whole point was to pit yourself against an opponent.

"Fine," said Gnash, shoving the page deeper into his pocket. "Me first."

The two boys took turns hitting fly balls to each other in the gathering dusk. Neither of them spoke. Gnash put everything he had into each swing, willing the ball to go past Jock's outstretched glove. He wanted to make the other boy feel the way he had felt when they'd had their fistfight. But Jock caught each ball as easily as if it had been thrown directly to him. He was always in the right spot, with his body fully in front of the ball and his glove ready.

Gnash was breathing heavily and he was sweaty with the exertion of swinging the bat as they changed places. Wordlessly, he ran past Jock to take his turn in the outfield.

As Jock tossed the ball into the air to hit it toward

the outfield, Gnash thought about the diagram. He had watched Jock's fly balls and he knew that they went hard and high. He also noticed that they tended toward the third-base line. He started shifting himself toward left field.

On the second ball, he noticed that the arcs of Jock's fly balls were farther out than he'd thought, so he took a couple of steps back. As he heard the metallic ring of bat against ball, he took two extra steps backward. It didn't feel right, but he knew from his Snickers wrapper that the highest point of the ball's arc would be farther out.

This time, when the ball came toward him, Gnash found that he barely had to move to catch it. He hopped left one step and then held his glove up and out from his chest. There was a satisfying slap as the ball landed in his glove.

"Like there's a magnet in my glove and the ball is metal," he whispered to himself.

12 COMMON GROUND

Gnash found himself making catches with a lot less effort. Instead of moving forward, he moved backward farther than he thought he needed to. Twice he had to run in to catch the ball, but he was nicely in position for nearly everything Jock belted out to him.

Sweat was pouring down his face. He barely noticed how tired he was when Jock yelled, "Hey, what do you think, last coupla balls?"

"Sure," Gnash said, realizing that it had gotten dark. Most of the people in the park had gone home.

"Hey, get really far back this time," Jock yelled.

Gnash backed up.

"No — farther," said Jock, waving his arm. "Farther!"

Gnash kept going until he was up against the fence. He shaded his eyes with one hand to block out the bright lights glaring down on the infield. He could see Jock behind home plate, but it didn't look like he was holding a bat. As Gnash watched, Jock coiled his body like a spring. Then Gnash saw the white ball screaming at him from the plate out to where he was standing — more than 230 feet away.

The ball went up and up. It looked like it would never come down. Finally it started to arc down, farther into the outfield than any of the balls either of them had batted. Gnash realized it was going to go past him.

As it sailed over him, Gnash jumped up as high as he could. His arms were stretched above his head but the ball neatly cleared him and kept going. Higher and higher and then — over the fence.

Gnash took off his cap and watched with amazement as the ball cleared the fence. It landed in the next diamond, rolling until it almost reached the pitcher's mound. Gnash stared at the ball, and then back toward Jock, practically a speck at the plate. Gnash laughed in surprise. Jock had thrown the ball farther than anyone Gnash had ever seen — even adults.

Gnash let out a *whoop*.

"Oh, sure, but can you do that again?" he called to Jock, teasingly.

Jock didn't answer, but instead coiled up and sent another ball heading toward Gnash, almost as high and nearly as fast. This time, however, it came down close enough that Gnash was able to catch it at the fence with a great leap in the air.

Gnash hopped the outfield fence and retrieved the first ball, still shaking his head in amazement. With two baseballs in his glove, he climbed back over the fence and ran to join Jock, who was sitting in the dugout, drinking a Gatorade.

For a moment, Gnash forgot how much he disliked Jock. "Holy crap!" he said, as he took off his glove and retrieved his water bottle. "Holy crap!"

Jock chuckled. "Pretty good party trick, eh?" he said.

"Yeah, how'd you do that?"

"I don't know," said Jock. "Just worked at it, I guess. Nothing else to do back home. I practised a lot."

"Well, it's pretty amazing. Shoot. I've got to hand it to you," said Gnash. He walked over to Jock and clunked bottles with him in a salute to his skill.

They drank, sitting beside each other, enjoying the silence of the Pits.

Finally Gnash spoke, "Hey, can I ask you something?"

"What?" asked Jock.

"What's it like?"

"What's what like?" asked Jock.

"You know. Being . . . the way you are."

"What, gay?" asked Jock.

"Yeah. Liking . . ." Gnash's voice trailed off.

"I don't know," said Jock, leaning against the dugout fence and taking a swig of his orange drink. "What's it like being straight?"

Gnash thought for a moment.

"I don't know," he said. "I don't really think about it. I've just always liked girls."

Jock motioned with his bottle toward Gnash. "Well, there you go," he said.

"What, you don't think about it?"

"Nope," said Jock. "I really don't think about it."

"Yeah, but . . . well, it's not normal, right?"

"It is for me," said Jock. "Look, what's a food you don't like?"

"Onions," said Gnash.

"And do you think about that?"

"I just avoid them."

"You didn't decide to hate onions. You didn't tell yourself, 'I'm never going to have onions,' right?"

"No."

"So," said Jock. "It's a bit like that — a preference that you've always had, even though other people have a different preference." Then he added, "Wait, that's a really stupid explanation."

"No, it's not," said Gnash. Then, "Actually, yeah. Yeah, it is." They both laughed. "Onions!"

They sat in silence, a slight smile on Gnash's face.

"I mean . . ." said Jock, thoughtfully, his voice trailing off.

"Yeah?"

"It's not like I've even been on a date or anything," said Jock.

"What?" Gnash was amazed.

Jock laughed. "Nope."

"Oh geez, I just assumed —"

"What?" asked Jock.

"I just figured you were, like, going out with all these guys and stuff . . ."

Jock laughed. "Is that what you're doing? Going out with girls all the time?"

"Oh, geez, no," said Gnash. "No, I haven't . . ."

Gnash stopped, about to say that he had never been on a date either. He chuckled.

"Honestly, I don't really do anything except base-ball," he said.

Jock laughed. "Me either," he said.

Suddenly, both boys jumped as a loud *clank* and then a *bzzzz* crackled overhead. In an instant, the floodlights went out. Darkness immediately descended on Christie Pits.

"I guess it's later than we thought," said Gnash, checking the time on his cell phone. He looked around the park. "Everyone's gone home."

"Yeah, time to go," said Jock, shifting on the bench to gather his things.

As the boys' eyes slowly grew used to the black-ness, they heard voices at the top of the hill. The voices got louder and Gnash and Jock saw three boys coming down the slope toward them.

"Hi, girls!" one boy called to them, in a horrible, sing-song voice. He waggled his fingers at them in a gesture that, in other circumstances, would have meant "hello." Tonight, it did not.

"Yeah," sneered another boy. "Hi, *ladies!*"

Jock and Gnash stared at the small but dangerous-looking gang headed their way.

13 HISTORY REPEATS

Gnash knew that soon he and Jock would be trapped. He stepped out of the dugout and stood at its entrance. The three boys came closer.

"Hey, Stretch, do you know what I heard?" one of the gang members asked his friends.

"No, what?" answered a lanky boy with blond curls.

"I heard that the new Blues kid likes *guys!*"

The lanky boy laughed. "You mean he's gay?"

"Yep, that's what I heard!"

Gnash could feel the blood rising in his face. He was more angry than afraid, even though it was dark and they were outnumbered. He stood in front of Jock, blocking him from the three boys.

"And you know what else I heard?" the boy asked Stretch. "That the Blues are losers! And you know who told me? Their *coach!*"

It was a ridiculous insult, but it fuelled Gnash's anger.

"Oh, yeah?" Gnash taunted back, "Well, at least we

can improve at baseball — you guys are *morons!* That'll *never* change!"

Stretch made a guttural sound in his throat and sprinted toward Gnash. All three boys closed in but Gnash had his fists up. He threw a punch at Stretch, connecting unevenly with part of his jaw. Then he shoved his shoulder against the other two boys, kicking out with his feet at the same time.

He wasn't thinking — raw anger had overtaken him. All he wanted to do was hurt the bullies.

Jock pushed his way to the entrance of the dugout and joined the fight, kicking and punching at the three boys. Gnash heard a grunt as one of the boys' fists connected with Jock's stomach.

Two of the boys were on the ground where Gnash had shoved them, but Stretch was still on his feet.

Jock became blocked in the dugout, behind the standoff that was happening between Gnash and Stretch. He turned and grabbed the only weapon he could find — a metal baseball bat.

Gnash looked around and snatched the bat from Jock. He waved it menacingly at Stretch, who stopped at the sight of it.

Gnash swung the bat hard against the metal pole at the entrance to the dugout. It made a horrible metallic clang that rang out across the dark, deserted Pits.

"Do you want to do this?" Gnash asked Stretch. He could feel himself losing control of his anger. "Because

I want to do this. Do you want to finish this?"

Stretch looked at his friends, lying in the dirt a few yards away. Their eyes were wide and fixed on the bat.

"Let's just get out of here," Jock whispered to Gnash. "Let's go." Something in Jock's voice pulled Gnash out of his angry trance.

Gnash looked at the bat in his hands and then over at the two boys. He realized Jock was right. They needed to get out of the park before something really bad happened.

"Who's the loser now?" Gnash asked, and he spat hard on the ground.

Gnash picked up Jock's baseball bag and shoved it into his arms, then grabbed his own. He pushed Jock roughly out of the dugout and along the fence. He heard Jock grunt as they headed away from the diamond. Still holding the bat up with one hand, Gnash walked slowly backward toward the slope of the hill, glaring at the other boys.

"*LOSERS!*" he screamed again. Then he turned, grabbed Jock's arm, and scrambled out of the diamond.

"Hey, where you *girls* going?" yelled one of the boys, who had finally clambered to his feet. With the angry, bat-wielding Gnash on the run he sounded a lot braver.

"Yeah, you *better* run!" called Stretch.

Gnash was very tempted to go back. He tightened his grip on the bat and turned toward the diamond. But Jock grabbed the back of his shirt and tugged him backward, clearly in a hurry to get away.

Jock and Gnash darted up the hill under the cover of the darkness. Gnash had spent countless hours going up and down the hills in the Pits, so his feet knew exactly where to plant themselves. He and Jock dragged each other upward, stumbling and slipping, until they reached the sidewalk at the top.

They could still hear the young thugs they'd left at the bottom of the Pits, yelling and running around the bases in the darkness.

Gnash and Jock hustled along the sidewalk and then darted down a nearby alley. They didn't stop until they were sure they weren't being followed. Both boys were breathing hard from their getaway. They stopped under a streetlight and Gnash looked at Jock, whose eyes were full and glistening.

"Holy crap," Gnash heard Jock say to himself. "*Holycrapholycrapholycrap.*"

Gnash didn't say a word. He put his baseball bag on the ground and unzipped it, placing the dented bat inside. He zipped it up again.

Jock's head was down and he was bent over, with his hands on his knees. Gnash could see his rib cage expanding and contracting with heavy breaths. It was a long time before Jock calmed down enough to stand up straight. He looked at Gnash, wide-eyed. "If you hadn't —" he started to say.

"Don't worry about it," said Gnash.

"But if they —"

"But they didn't," said Gnash.

"I mean, stuff has happened to me before, but that was just *crazy*!" said Jock. "They wanted to —"

"They wouldn't have done anything," said Gnash. "And you know why?"

"Why?" asked Jock.

"Because we know where they live," said Gnash.

"We know where they live?" asked Jock. "What do you mean, we know where they live?"

"Those jerks were Pirates," said Gnash gruffly. "The Parkhill kind."

***

Gnash slowly climbed the stairs up to his apartment, his mind going over what had happened in the Pits. He'd watched Jock's bus lumber down the street. He could still see the raw fear on Jock's face as he'd stared out at Gnash from the window of the bus.

His own fear had quickly turned to anger. All he could think about was what he would do to the three Pirates who had tormented his friend. *Friend*, Gnash realized with a start. He wondered when he'd started thinking about Jock that way.

He didn't have long to think about it.

"Nash Calvecchio, get in here!" his grandfather's voice thundered down the hall.

What now? Gnash wondered.

Gnash set his baseball bag down and slowly walked into the small living room. His grandfather was pointing at the clock on the wall above the TV. "What time do you call this?" he demanded.

"We were practising," Gnash said. His voice sounded squeaky to his own ears.

"Practising? The coach called a practice at this time of night? That's it, that's ridiculous — I'm gonna call him!" his grandfather said, reaching for the phone.

"No, it wasn't everyone," said Gnash.

"Well, who, then?" asked his grandfather, coming closer.

"It was just a couple of us," said Gnash. He realized tears were welling up behind his eyes and he felt his face grow hot.

"Well, it's not fair to your grandmother, coming in at this time of night!" Gnash's grandfather's voice boomed.

Gnash suddenly felt bone-tired. His mind searched for a way to get away from his grandfather without making him angrier. He just wanted a safe, quiet, comfortable space to think. He wanted to crawl into his bed and sleep.

But it was more than half an hour before Gnash would be able to do that. Half an hour of keeping his tears in check so he didn't cry in front of his grandfather. Half an hour of waiting until he could get away.

Finally, his grandfather grew tired of his own bluster and Gnash found his moment. He faded backward into the hallway and slipped into his room. He closed the door without a sound and sank onto his bed. He stretched out on his mattress and let go of the tears he had been holding back, making sure that his sobs wouldn't be overheard.

Gnash didn't know why he was crying. It felt like every sob was being wrung out of him, like a dishrag. His tears felt like part anger and part relief. He turned over and buried his face in his pillow.

14 DISAPPEARING ACT

The next day, the Blues were sitting in the lunchroom at their table, doing their usual sandwich-trades. Sebastian was eating a sandwich that was half tuna and half salami. It looked exactly like Tami's sandwich.

Since Jock had joined the team, lunchtime was a bit more restrained. But this afternoon, Jock wasn't at the table.

"Was Jock in homeroom this morning, Gnash?" Sebastian asked.

"What do I look like, the guy's secretary?" Gnash grumbled.

"Come to think of it, I didn't see him at the lockers before school this morning or before lunch," said Sebastian.

"What classes did you guys have this morning?" Raj asked Gnash.

"Computer, History, Health," mumbled Gnash over a mouthful of macaroni salad.

"You're doing Health already?" Sebastian asked, bits

of sandwich falling out of his mouth. "Suck-*ahs*! We don't start that until next week. We're still finishing up basketball."

"Do you know where he is?" Raj asked Gnash. "Look, if you know something, just tell us."

"What the heck?!" asked Gnash, so loudly that the kids at the next table stopped their conversation and looked over at them. "I didn't do anything. I didn't see anything. I don't know anything. I have no idea where the American is."

"Oh, well, he's probably at a dentist appointment or something," said Raj. "Too bad. I wanted to talk to him about the Pirates game this weekend. I'll just text him." Raj brought out his phone and thumbed a message. Cell phones were allowed during off-periods like lunch.

When Raj didn't hear back, he sent another text.

There was no answer back from Jock by the end of lunch.

"That's so *weird*," said Raj.

"You mean it's weird that Jock isn't texting you back?" asked Tami.

"Well, that and your *sandwich* is weird," said Raj.

"Hey, I'm very proud of that sandwich," said Tami. "It contained nearly all of the food groups!"

Gnash got up to leave the cafeteria. "If His Royal Highness puts in an appearance during Geography class, is there a message?" he asked in a broad accent that sounded more German than British.

"Yes," said Raj. "Tell him I wanna talk to him."

"I will have *my people* deliver the message," said Gnash with an exaggerated bow, and he strode out of the cafeteria.

But Jock wasn't in class the next period, or the one after that. During the last period of the day, the principal showed up at the classroom and signalled to the teacher to come to the door. After a brief chat, she poked her head into the room and crooked a finger at Gnash, calling him into the hall.

Gnash rolled his eyes. What was he going to get blamed for now? he wondered.

The principal's lips were pinched in disapproval.

"Nash, have you seen Jock today?" she asked.

"Why is everyone asking me that?" asked Gnash, exasperated. "I haven't seen the guy!"

"Is that the truth?" she asked. Her eyes told Gnash that there was something she wasn't saying about Jock's absence.

"Why? Where is he?" asked Gnash.

He wanted to know what the principal wasn't telling him.

"He's on my ball team, eh?" said Gnash. "We're teammates. I'd like to know what's going on."

"Oh?" She seemed surprised. "He's on your baseball team?"

"Yes."

She sighed. "I got a call from his mother this afternoon. Some kids have been bothering Jock. We are taking it very seriously."

"What do you mean, bothering?" asked Gnash. "Like, bullying?"

"Yes. Apparently he was in Christie Pits and a number of boys were bullying him."

"Yeah," said Gnash. "Yeah, I can believe that."

He knew he was holding back important information, but he didn't want anyone to think of him as a victim who got bullied. Worse, he didn't want his principal telling his grandfather that he had nearly been beaten up by a bunch of rich kids. That wouldn't go over well.

"I didn't realize you two were teammates," she said. "I'm glad Jock has some friends to watch out for him."

"Well, of course," said Gnash.

"He's going to need friends right now. I hate it when this kind of thing happens. Bullies."

"Yeah," said Gnash thoughtfully. "Me, too."

Gnash realized that he really did dislike bullies. Bullies like the kids who couldn't let another kid just take his time getting down a slide. Bullies like the teachers who told kids that they couldn't talk or text or even get up and stretch their legs during class.

A shadow passed over Gnash's face. Bullies like his grandfather, who made him feel like he needed to get a home run or he was no good. Who held back their smiles and hugs for a kid's "own good." Who always insisted it was their job to teach a kid "a lesson" — but that lesson was always terrible.

Bullies who weren't happy letting people just be who they were. Bullies who had to put a guy down for being different.

Bullies, it slowly, horribly, dawned on Gnash, *like himself.*

15 DISCUSSION AT HOME

Later that day, Gnash was still thinking about how he had been bullying Jock when he saw Raj in the hall. Suddenly, he knew what he needed to do.

"Hey Raj," he said, "I think we need to go find Jock — what do you think?"

"I was thinking the same thing," said Raj.

"Let's meet at our lockers after school and head over to his house," said Raj.

"Do you know where he lives?" asked Gnash.

"No, but I'll find out," said Raj. "I'm sure Coop knows. I'll talk him into telling me."

After the final bell rang, the two boys threw their books into their lockers, grabbed their cell phones and headed to the bus stop. They rode the bus west for a few blocks and then transferred to a second one headed south.

"Jock lives pretty far from the school, eh?" said Gnash as they climbed out at the bus stop.

"Yeah, I didn't realize," said Raj.

The boys walked up to a high-rise apartment building that looked like it had seen better days. The paint was peeling off in chunks from the balconies and the front door to the building was jammed open. They went inside and headed to the elevator, where they pushed the button for the twelfth floor.

In the elevator Gnash crinkled his nose. "Smells like feet," he said.

Raj took a deep breath. "Mmmm, I do love that delectable *feet* smell," he laughed.

When the elevator doors opened, it was onto a dingy grey hallway, dimly lit by lights hanging from the wall. Each one was at a different angle. They walked down the hall until they found apartment 1208 and knocked on the door. There was the sound of steps and then scuffling, as though someone was peering at them through the peephole in the door. They heard the lock being turned and the door opened.

"Hey, guys," said Jock. His eyes were puffy and he was wearing pajamas and a threadbare blue robe. His bare feet shuffled backward as he drew back the door and invited them in. "What's up? Hey, how'd you know where I live?"

"Coo—" Gnash started to say, until Raj interrupted him. "I told the principal we had to bring you your homework." Gnash suddenly realized that the coach might get in trouble for giving out a team member's home address.

Jock motioned for them to sit at the kitchen table which, although spotless, was clearly well used. They pulled up chairs.

Jock went to the fridge and pulled out three cans of pop. There were loud hisses as they opened their drinks.

"So, how come you weren't in school today?" Gnash asked. He took a long swig and then burped loudly.

"I had to go the hospital and get an X-ray of my arm," said Jock. "I kinda ripped it open the other night down at the Pits."

"Huh?" said Raj, confused. "What were you doing at the Pits?"

"Gnash didn't tell you?" asked Jock.

"Tell me what?" asked Raj.

Both boys turned to look at Gnash, who was sitting with one leg slung over the arm of his chair, silently sipping his drink.

"We had a little . . . thing," said Gnash.

"A little thing? A little *thing*!?" said Jock, leaning forward in his chair. "We coulda been killed!"

"Well, now you're exaggerating," said Gnash, calmly. "Anyway, I've got it under control. I've got a plan."

"What are you guys talking about?" said Raj.

"You didn't tell him? I can't believe you didn't tell him!" said Jock.

"There's nothing to tell," said Gnash. "It was a *thing*. It was nothing."

"Well, it wasn't *nothing* to me," said Jock.

"Will someone please tell me what's going on?" asked Raj shrilly. "Gnash, what did you do?"

"See, this is why I don't like telling people stuff," said Gnash, his face getting red. "I knew it. You think I did something. I get blamed for everything!" He started to get up from the chair.

"Hold on, Gnash, nobody's blaming you for anything," said Jock.

"Well, I am," said Raj, heatedly. "You've been pushing Jock around ever since he got here. Everyone knows you don't like him. Everyone knows you're homophobic."

Gnash's face went white. He couldn't believe that his best friend thought he was capable of hurting Jock.

"Wait, Raj," said Jock, jumping in and preventing Gnash from leaving. "It's not like that. Sit down, Gnash. Raj, listen."

Jock told Raj the whole story, from the unplanned practice with Gnash, to the incident with the Pirates and how Gnash had stuck up for Jock.

After Jock stopped talking, there was silence.

Raj was the first one to speak. "Holy cow," he said quietly. "Gnash, I'm really sorry."

"Whatever," said Gnash, his eyes narrowed and focussed on Raj.

"Oh, geez, Jock," said Raj. "Is that what happened to your arm?"

"Well, that part actually *was* Gnash's fault," Jock said, looking at Gnash.

"What the—?!" said Gnash, standing up again.

Then Jock laughed. "No, remember when you shoved me out of the dugout?" he said. "I bashed my arm against the fence. Look."

Jock rolled up the sleeve of his tattered dressing gown to reveal a deep scrape and a dark, purple bruise about ten centimetres long. "I must have caught it on a piece of wire," he said. "At the time, I didn't even feel it. I just wanted to get out of there."

"Anyway, I had it X-rayed and they gave me some kind of needle, and it's fine," he said. "I'm good to play tomorrow. The Pirates, right?" Jock shot a knowing look at Gnash.

"But I don't get why you never told us," said Raj. "Or why you didn't return any of our texts."

"My cell plan expired," explained Jock. "My phone's dead. At least, until I get some money umpiring house league or something to pay for a phone card."

"Yeah, well, next time let someone know, eh?" said Raj. "And that goes for both of you," he said, turning on Gnash. "You're part of a team."

"Yeah, well, maybe it doesn't feel that way sometimes," Gnash mumbled, staring into his drink.

"What you send out into the universe comes back at you, man," said Raj. "It comes back."

Gnash didn't reply.

And then Raj added, "Listen, what you did for Jock — that's gonna come back to you, too."

"Yeah, I didn't really get a chance to thank you, Gnash," said Jock. "It's not too often that someone has my back like that."

Gnash sat silently. Finally he said, in a voice just barely audible to the other boys, "Well, all I know is that those rich losers have got it coming."

It took some time for Jock and Raj to convince Gnash not to seek revenge on the Parkhill Pirates who had bullied them. Jock said Gnash couldn't go through life trying to get back at every ignorant jerk — there were too many of them.

But it was Raj's comment that broke through. "The best way to show these guys is on the field," he said. "Beat them at baseball. Beat them badly. It's the only way."

That made a lot of sense to Gnash.

"Our next game decides who goes to the provincials," Raj said. "There's one spot left. It's either gonna go to us or to the Pirates."

"It's got to be us!" Gnash said.

"Then . . ." said Raj.

"Let's get 'em," said Gnash.

"Yeah," said Raj. "We win this one, and the Pirates' season is finished."

"*Schzeeeeet!*" said Gnash, making a cutting gesture across his throat. "Game over."

16 BATTLE IN THE PITS

On the diamond, fifteen minutes before the game, Raj was on the pitcher's mound squinting toward home plate.

Gnash jogged out to centre field. Once there, he looked around the outfield and then bent down and picked up a hot dog wrapper that had blown over from the nearby snack bar. He scrunched it up and then, carefully picking his spot, set it down on the grass. He stood near the wrapper and looked toward home plate, then up into the sky. Then he bent down again and moved the wrapper about a foot to the right. He jogged back to the dugout.

Jock was sitting at the far end of the dugout, away from the entrance. He was absentmindedly rubbing his arm, which was wrapped in a beige stretchy bandage. He jumped at the sound of Gnash walking in.

"Sorry," said Gnash.

"No . . . no problem," said Jock. "I'm a bit on edge."

"Yeah. Hey, I thought your arm was all right," Gnash said, gesturing to the bandage.

"It is. It was bleeding a bit earlier, that's all. I'm fine to play."

There was an awkward silence. They both looked toward the Visitors' bench, where some of the Pirates were lined up. Seeing Stretch talking to the Pirates' coach, Gnash's eyes narrowed and he scowled.

"Are you sure you don't want me to —"

"No, Gnash," Jock cut him off.

"I mean, I could just get him alone and —"

"Gnash, stop! You're not going to do anything to them," said Jock.

Gnash ran his fingers through his hair and then shoved his cap down over his eyes. Jock held Gnash's angry glance until finally Gnash laughed. "Okay, okay!" he said, putting his hands up.

But then he backtracked.

"Not even just one little —"

"No! Not even 'just one little' anything! Number one, I don't need you to fight my battles for me. And number two, this is a battle that we need to fight out *there*," said Jock, pointing with his thumb toward the field.

"Yeah, that's a given," said Gnash. "They're going down."

"They're going down," agreed Jock, nodding.

Coop stuck his head into the dugout. "Okay, guys," he said. "Let's get out there."

Jock grabbed his glove and headed onto the field

but Gnash stayed behind. "Hey, Coop, can I talk to you real quick?" he asked.

"Hurry," said Coop. "We're already on the field."

"Coop, can I play centre? Just this one game? Jock can take my spot at short. Please."

Coop looked at Gnash, surprised. He had never asked his coach anything remotely like this before.

"Just this once," Coop said. "Go ahead."

Gnash brightened. "Great!" he said over his shoulder as he ran onto the field. "I'll tell Jock!"

As Gnash ran by Jock to switch places with him, they both jumped up for a high high-five.

"Play ball!" yelled the umpire, and the game began.

The first two batters went by quickly, in just eight pitches, with two of the Pirates ending up on base.

Gnash recognized the next batter as one of the bullies who had threatened them in the Pits. His eyes narrowed as he watched the boy take two practice swings and then step into the batter's box. Gnash felt his face grow hot with anger. He looked around to judge the distance between himself and the infield — and then he jogged backward a few yards, closer to the wrapper he had placed on the ground. He took two more steps back, and then got into his ready position.

When the boy's pop fly came toward him, Gnash held out his glove. He was perfectly in position and the ball seemed to be pulled right into his hands. *Like a magnet*, thought Gnash, as the umpire called, "Caught!"

With a smile, Gnash tossed the ball to Jock, who threw it in to Raj.

Stretch was the Pirates' best player, and he'd been put in the clean-up spot, number four on the batting roster. As he came up to bat, the air in the infield seemed to crackle. All of the Blues knew what Stretch and his teammates had done to Gnash and Jock. They had all agreed on their goals: first, win the game. Second, prevent Stretch and the other two bullies from scoring.

When Stretch approached the batter's box, the Pirates had a player on second and a player on third. Stretch smiled smugly at Raj on the mound. Before stepping in, he turned toward Jock and, holding one hand up in the air, casually waggled his fingers. For a minute, Gnash found it difficult to concentrate on the game.

He took a moment to get control of his anger, and then yelled, "C'mon Raj! You can do it! Let's strike this guy out!"

There were calls and jeers from all of the Blues in the field as they echoed Gnash's sentiments. "Let's get him!" Miguel called. "You can do it, Raj! All you, buddy! You *got* this!"

Raj was clearly shaken by having to pitch to Stretch. Out in centre field, Gnash could tell that Raj was nervous. Raj turned and looked at the runners. When he was satisfied that they were staying put, he wound up.

The ball was faster and harder than anything Raj

had ever thrown. Unfortunately for the loudmouthed batter, it was low and way inside. When the fastball made contact with Stretch's thigh, the big boy landed hard on the ground and he didn't get up.

Gnash thumped his fist into his glove.

"You did that on purpose!" Stretch yelled, still lying on the ground and furiously rubbing his left leg. "He did that on purpose!" he said to the umpire and pointing at Raj.

The look on Raj's face clearly indicated that he had not. Coop called, "Time!"

Jock ran in to the mound before Coop could get there.

"Hey, Raj, it's okay, man," he said.

"I swear I didn't do that on purpose!" Raj said, watching Stretch limp to first.

"Did you check your front foot?" asked Jock.

"No, I didn't," said Raj. His face was as white as the chalk lines on the field. "That guy's such a jerk!"

"I know," said Jock. "I know. Let's just get him out." He went back to his position.

The bases were loaded.

"Play ball!" yelled the umpire, to get the game started again.

"You got this, Raj," Gnash called.

Raj settled onto the rubber again and checked his footing.

The Pirates' batter settled into his stance and loaded up.

Raj looked at the batter, and then straightened up and stepped off the rubber. He flexed his shoulders. The batter relaxed and knocked the head of his bat against the bottom of his cleats. Raj moved back to the rubber and went down into his pitching stance again, looking over at first base and then third before putting his ball-hand into his glove.

He looked down at his feet and then pulled his arm all the way back. When he brought it forward, letting the ball go, it was hard, low and directly over the plate.

"Strike!" yelled the ump.

His second pitch was wide of the plate, but the next pitch was perfectly placed.

"Strike!" the umpire said again. He held up his fingers and gave the count, "one and two."

Raj was in the middle of his wind-up when the field umpire behind him suddenly put one hand up. "*Balk!*" he said.

Raj held out his arms in a gesture of confusion and looked over at Coop, who asked for time and then crossed the baseline onto the field toward the umpire.

The batter smirked in the box as he watched the umpire and the coach argue about whether Raj had, in fact, *balked* — stopped in the middle of his pitch.

The conversation on the mound ended and the umpire motioned for the boy on first base to go to second, the penalty for Raj's balk. Since the bases were loaded, that brought the boy on third home. The Pirates' fans whistled and hooted as the runner crossed home plate.

The Pirates were leading 1–0.

"That's okay, Raj," yelled Gnash. "Shake it off!" The other Blues chimed in with "shake it off" and "we'll get it back!" Raj took a deep breath.

He went back into his stance. He checked his feet and then wound up and threw the ball hard over the plate. The umpire's call, "Strike!" took the smirk off the batter's face and he returned to his dugout, dragging his bat along the ground.

17 DOUBLE PLAY

For the rest of the game, every time Jock came up to bat the Pirates started chanting, "*heyboy, heyboy, heyboy!*" in high-pitched singsong voices.

Gnash could tell that the Pirates thought they were throwing punches at Jock's weak spot. But Gnash knew that being gay wasn't Jock's weak spot.

"That noise just sounds like ignorance to me," said Jock to Gnash over the Pirates' hollers. "And that's on them, not me."

Now, approaching the seventh inning with the score tied, Gnash, Raj, Tami and the rest of the Blues were feeling more like a team than they ever had before. They were hanging tough — together. They wanted to wipe the field with the Pirates, and three Pirates in particular.

Raj had managed to pitch four strong innings, but he'd run out his pitch-count and had to be relieved. Tami came in to close the game, but she was having trouble finding the strike zone. She'd walked Stretch, so at the top of the final inning, he was on first.

And then it happened.

Stretch had taken a long lead off the base and was down in a running stance, staring at Jock. Stretch waggled his fingers at him again and again, going back and forth to the base and then taking another lead-off.

Finally, when the crack of the bat signalled a hit, Stretch put his head down and charged. But Stretch wasn't heading for the base. He was heading for Jock. Stretch plowed into Jock with his full body weight before rebounding off him and rolling toward the base.

The umpire stepped in, but it was too late. Jock was on the ground holding his bandaged arm. Stretch was smiling smugly.

"Yer out!" yelled the umpire, holding up one fist and gesturing toward Stretch.

The tall boy slowly got to his feet and looked at Jock. He smirked. "That's okay — Rani is gonna bring in the winning run," he said, gesturing to the girl on first.

Then the umpire added, "And *you're* out!" to Rani.

Both coaches headed out to the mound to talk to the umpire. It was Jock's turn to smirk.

Coop called the team to the mound to explain that the umpire was throwing two Pirates out for "charging." He said that if Stretch hadn't charged Jock, the Blues would have had an easy double play. Stretch had cost the Pirates two runners instead of one and closed the top of the seventh inning.

Over in the Pirates' dugout, Gnash could see the players turning their anger on a different enemy — their own teammate. Stretch was no longer grinning.

In the bottom of the final inning, Gnash handed Sebastian the bat. It was the Blues' last chance to win the game and take the team to the provincials. They needed one run to win the game, and end the Pirates' season.

In the batter's box, Sebastian nervously eyed the pitcher, who threw the ball hard and fast straight down the middle. Sebastian swung late, his body momentum carrying him awkwardly forward.

"Strike!" the umpire said.

The next two balls got by Sebastian as well. He angrily clomped back to the dugout, kicking the dirt on the way.

"One out," said Coop anxiously.

They needed a run. Just one run.

Gnash was up next. He adjusted his glove strap and then stepped into the batter's box. He looked over at Jock in the on-deck circle, who nodded.

The pitch was hard and fast. All Gnash had to do was stick out his bat. It connected with the ball for a straight hit that streaked up the middle. The pitcher flung himself to one side as the ball whizzed past him and flew out to the grass. The outfielder charged at it and then sent it to the third baseman.

But it was a big enough hit for Gnash to get to

second. He stood, panting, with one foot on the base, watching as Jock left the on-deck circle and walked to the plate.

Stretch had been benched by his coach for his unsportsmanlike conduct. Still, his jeers were easily the loudest in the ballpark as Jock entered the batter's box. "*Heyboy, heyboy, heyboy,*" called Stretch.

Jock didn't bother looking over. He crouched down and loaded up his bat.

The first pitch went by. "*Strike!*"

Gnash looked over at Coop and it occurred to him that their coach might actually faint, he looked so nervous. Gnash crouched lower, getting ready to run to third.

But the second pitch went by Jock, too.

The third one did not.

Jock found a big piece of the ball and cracked it with everything he had. The ball went up into the air, spinning high and white above the Pits. Jock took off for first.

Three of the Pirates dashed toward the ball in the outfield, their gloves up in the air. They were yelling at each other to back off. Their necks were craned so they could focus on the ball that was dropping like a rock into centre field. None of them backed off, and the three players came together with a crunch.

The ball dropped onto the grass between them.

The Blues' parents cheered. Jock continued running

to second base, pushing Gnash ahead of him to third, before one of the Pirates picked up the ball and sent it in to stop the runners.

"Time!" yelled the Pirates' coach, striding out to talk to his team.

Gnash took advantage of the time-out. He called Jock over.

"Jock, I've got an idea," he whispered, making sure the Pirates couldn't overhear him.

Coop watched from the dugout impatiently. He paced back and forth along the third-base line, alternately spitting on the ground and running his hand through his hair.

When Gnash had finished explaining, he held out his fist. Jock bumped it, and then jogged back to second.

Miguel came up to bat. Gnash had one foot on third and his eye on the pitcher, who went into his wind-up. As the pitcher's front leg came up and his arm came forward to launch the ball, Gnash pushed off from third. He was going to steal home.

"Strike!" yelled the umpire, as the baseball went *thunk* into the catcher's mitt. But it was too late for Gnash. His momentum was already carrying him toward home plate. His feet slid on the dry dirt and his arms cartwheeled backward as he saw that the catcher had the ball.

Gnash backed up and twisted around to run back to third, with the catcher hot on his heels. The catcher threw the ball to the third baseman, who closed in on Gnash from the other side. He held out the ball to tag Gnash as he ran forward. Gnash turned again and ran the other way, back toward home. He'd only run two steps, when the ball was sent to another Pirate, who closed in. The boy took one step and Gnash knew he was doomed. He felt the ball touch his back. He was tagged out.

The crowd on the Pirates' side clapped and hooted as the umpire made the call. Over the din, Stretch's terrible, mocking voice was the loudest of all. Three of the Pirates were jumping in the air high-fiving each other along the third-base line, as Gnash walked slowly back to the dugout.

And then suddenly, there was a commotion along the third-base line. Gnash turned to watch Jock round third base and blow right past the celebrating Pirates.

The Pirates looked at each other in confusion. The Blues started cheering and the Pirates on the bench began screaming at their players to throw the ball, "*Home! Home!*" But it was too late.

"*SAFE!*" yelled the umpire, as Jock slid into home, kicking up an enormous cloud of dust, to score the winning run.

For a moment, no one could quite figure out what had happened. And then a great cheer went up from the stands behind the Blues' bench. Gnash, Sebastian, Miguel and the rest of the Blues ran toward Jock and slammed into him, high-fiving and throwing their gloves in the air.

"We won! We won! *We won!*" Sebastian yelled over and over again as he and the others laughed and jumped up and down.

Coop chuckled in relief, and spit out a mouthful of seeds. "Those two planned the whole thing," he said, grinning. "Unbelievable."

The cheering and jumping and piling on continued for at least ten minutes. Tami ran over and picked up Gnash in an enthusiastic bear hug.

"Put me down, you nut-job," Gnash said, but Tami had already run off to hug someone else.

Gnash's face darkened as he caught sight of his grandfather half-way up the hill on his way out of the park. Gnash was certain that his grandfather would be angry at him for helping a boy like Jock. He would never understand. Gnash hung his head, suddenly deflated. He was about to walk away when his grandfather turned and caught his eye. He held up his hand, beckoning Josh over.

"That was a smart play," Gnash's grandfather said as Gnash joined him on the hill. "And, boy, was I glad you wiped the smirk off that rich jerk's face. Nash, I'm proud of you."

Gnash didn't have long to consider his grandfather's words, because Sebastian and Raj suddenly launched themselves at him, knocking him sideways on the hill.

"Hey, man," said Raj, ruffling Gnash's hair, "great job."

"YEAH!" said Sebastian, running up the hill and yelling as though everyone around him was deaf. "GREAT JOB! *WOO-HOO!*"

Gradually, they were joined by the other Blues, who had packed up their baseball bags and were lugging them up the steep incline. Gnash patted Jock on the back and put his arm around him. "Hey, welcome to the team."

Just then, the sky began to darken over the Pits. The players heard rumblings in the distance and drops of rain began to fall. Before long, sheets of water were dousing the kids on the hill, which was quickly becoming a muddy, slippery stream.

Sebastian, who was at the top of the hill, turned and looked down at his teammates.

"*MUDBALL!*" he shouted, his voice cracking in excitement.

The teammates dropped their bags. Sebastian launched his rolling body down the hill, first careening into Jock and then Tami, Raj and Gnash.

The players scattered like bowling pins, a heap of muddy, laughing bodies — a team.

ACKNOWLEDGEMENTS

This is my first novel and there are many people who helped to make it possible.

Carolyn, who lovingly devoured the book, encouraged me relentlessly — and then helped me get the baseball scenes just right.

Bennett, for creating the game of Mudball and for showing me what it looks like when you truly love the sport of baseball.

Angela, who helped me focus the plot — and lots of other stuff.

Kat, my awesome editor, who took it all up a notch.

Ryan (Army) Armstrong, pitching coach at The Baseball Zone in Mississauga, for pointing Raj's front foot forward.

Val, WTW, Paul and Gord for their encouragement and support.

My mom, who sells more of my books than anyone.

My in-person writing group and #write-o-rama, my virtual one.

Cathie, Katie, Stephanie, Julie, John and Scott, who made the book better.

All of the talented and supportive people at Lorimer.

Christie (yes, as in Christie Pits), the first one to know that I could write this book.

Karen, for a Post-It that I will never lose.

Coach Coop, who lent his expertise and his name

Acknowledgements

— and who does *not* have a faux-hawk.

The Toronto Playgrounds and North York Blues organizations — the coaches, parents and, of course, players, who provided invaluable expertise, support and inspiration.

And as always, Andrew, my rock.

★★★

I'm grateful to The Ontario Arts Council for their financial support in aiding me research and write this book.

Christie Pits is one of my favourite places in Toronto, and there really was a riot there in 1933. Other than that, all of the places, events, teams, schools and players in this book are fictional.

★★★

These resources helped me get my facts straight:

The Baseball Codes: Beanballs, Sign Stealing, and Bench-Clearing Brawls: The Unwritten Rules of America's Pastime. 2011. By Jason Turbow and Michael Duca.

The Riot at Christie Pits. 1987. By Cyril Levitt.

"The Christie Pits riot," *Wikipedia*.

MORE SPORTS, MORE ACTION
www.lorimer.ca/sportsstories

CHECK OUT THESE OTHER BASEBALL STORIES FROM LORIMER'S SPORTS STORIES SERIES:

CURVE BALL
by John Danakas

Tom Poulos is looking forward to a summer of baseball. But instead of playing catcher for the Jarvis Badgers, Tom finds himself on a plane to Winnipeg, where he'll spend the summer with an uncle he doesn't even know.

"Fun and immensely enjoyable . . . Ball fans will enjoy this book."

— Quill & Quire

DOUBLE PLAY
by Sara Cassidy

Allie's invited to play on the boy's baseball team but then her step-brother announces he wants to play on the girl's team!

Commended — A Junior Library Guild Selection
Commended — Canadian Children's Book Centre Best Books for
Kids and Teens Starred Section

POWER HITTER
by Christine A. Forsyth

Conner might need a pinch runner, pinch catcher, and pinch thrower, but can he ever hit a baseball out of the park! So when Connor ends up with his baseball-loving family in Winnipeg for the summer, he allows his cousin to talk him into trying out for the team.

Commended — Canadian Children's Book Centre Best Books for Kids and Teens Section